# EDEN

❧❧

## A NOVEL
WITH A LOT OF TRUTH TO IT

D. KEVIN MAY, PH.D.

**Outskirts Press, Inc.**
**Denver, Colorado**

For additional information, visit www.kev.net.

ISBN: 978-1-4327-2133-6

Outskirts Press, Inc.
http://www.outskirtspress.com

Outskirts Press and the "OP" logo are trademarks belonging to Outskirts Press, Inc.

Scripture taken from or adapted from the King James Version of the Bible.

Scripture taken from the HOLY BIBLE, NEW INTERNATIONAL VERSION®. NIV®. Copyright© 1973, 1978, 1984 by International Bible Society. Used by permission of Zondervan. All rights reserved.

Special thanks to Jeanette Gerke and Bethany Thier for their editorial excellence.

**To:**

You.

# prologue

*Just keep driving.*

Those words have provoked me since awarded my ticket to autonomy at the age of sixteen, an Ohio driver's license. That entitlement was my escape, the vessel destined to lift me from pain and deliver me to distinction. You see, freedom has always been my unending pursuit and *just keep driving* my mantra.

At first, in times of trouble and doubt, *just keep driving* would chauffeur me from conflict on the home front, leverage me from lifestyle standoffs and was the means of dodging fallout from my transgressions. It worked like a charm. Given its success in handling discord, it wasn't long before *just keep driving* became my oracle, my song of freedom – the battle cry of my restless, revolutionary spirit.

Something extraordinary happened along the way. – I got what I asked for. And you know what they say. *Don't ask for what you want, because you just might get it.* So with each new dream fulfilled, my entrapment to *just keep driving* persists.

Hello, my friend. Thanks for inviting me into your life to share my story. I've needed to admit this for some time. However, there were demons to deal with and battles to be fought. Damn demons, they just seem to get in the way of whatever we set out to accomplish. So here I am, years later, humbly prepared to confess.

It's a frightening proposition to be entirely open with a friend. Nevertheless, I've found delving into one's own soul a more disturbing compulsion. But that's what I had to do. Be shamefully honest with *me* to be fully open with *you*.

The impetus for my act of contrition transpired during a weekend getaway back in 2005. To be precise, the events occurred on July 22nd through the 25th in and around the seductive city of Lugano, Switzerland. Since those days, some have said I became like a gypsy on a lengthy sojourn destined for demise. Admittedly I was a nomad of sorts, on a trek to no place in particular. Choosing to live without a clock or compass.

However, that really wasn't the case. Now it's evident I was in training, like that of a soldier being prepared for battle.

My personal *Jihad.*

I realize once I share my story with you, my life will no longer be my own. You see, it's like making a deal with the dark side. Once you go down that path there's no turning back. It was a difficult decision, but one I had to make.

The story you are about to read is true. The events actually happened as described, with varying degrees of accuracy. I chose to write this as a novel for the freedom to dramatize where necessary, that way, offering you a complete portrayal of what actually happened. In some cases I've slipped in a little fiction, usually based in part on *some* reality, just to spice things up.

Characterizations of individuals I've met along the way will serve as the people you meet in the coming pages. Not all characters are true to life. Actually, many are not. One character, however, is presented exactly as he represented himself – Silvio. With that said, you can have complete faith that the source of my words is founded in absolute truth.

As you turn the page to embark on this journey, promise to stay with me until the very end. This mission necessitates that level of commitment. You see, some truths are not fully revealed until you reach your destination.

Your destiny.

As we take these steps together, stay alert. Perhaps even vigilant. Deceit, if packaged properly, can be very alluring. Be forewarned, the wisdom of a fool will not set you free.

Regardless of the gravity of my passage, be assured we're gonna have a good time. Life is an amazing adventure. I'm one to embrace the moment, to fully open myself to the prospect of unexpected delights. It would be sinful not to raise a little hell along the way.

Finally, I am *not* a teacher. This is not an effort to manipulate or induce you into my way of viewing the world. Our views are our own; a matter of personal choice, free will. I simply hope to inspire and to challenge; to promote sincere self-evaluation. I want to offer you something that encourages discussion and debate, something that will open a new channel of communication between each one of us.

It's time we begin to share the knowledge that has been conferred upon *each one of us*.

> *This is our challenge.*
> *This is our revolution.*
> *This is our destiny…*

> *Just keep driving.*

In a world divided, a new revolution is our only hope.

# chapter one

"Our world has changed, my friend."

The stranger's words echoed between the pallid green walls that engulfed the vacant platform and the lone train awaiting its departure for the two hour journey through the Italian Alps.

"Our world has changed and there is nothing you can do about it!"

Shaken from the comfort of my reflective trance, my eyes shot upward from their intense focus on the dancing flame being pulled from my lighter to the cigarette hanging from my lips. A single torrent of blinding sunlight splashed across my face as the beam completed its path down the station steps to the lower platform where I had been standing in solitude. Squinting through the blaring light that served as a backdrop for the swirling smoke just exhaled from my last cigarette before departure, my sight captured a silhouette of the offender who had thoughtlessly invaded my silence.

"It's *the challenge!*" he declared, bounding toward me with the grace of a jack-in-the-box clown bouncing and swaying on his spring.

As my eyes adjusted to the light, I could see the face of a lanky fellow. He looked to be in his mid-fifties; his cheeks were sallow and drawn. His face, tired. Harsh lines ran vertically from his chins to his elongated ears. Tufts of gray protruded out either side of his head, crowned by a shiny hairless dome. His nearly complete set of teeth sparkled as he freely smiled. His thick, dark eyebrows bounced in rhythm as he spoke. His voice was robust, his American English, nearly native, with barely the hint of an indistinguishable accent.

"Take that cigarette, for example," he said while moving increasingly closer, "We can no longer smoke our cigarettes on the trains in Italy. What right do they have? Little by little, every freedom we have will belong to them!"

Processing the arrival of this gauntly character, a picture of Michael Keaton as *Beetlejuice* flashed in my head. There was no stopping the immense smile that fought its way onto my face, as a result of self-amusement. He was Beetlejuice; in all his doom, he still possessed a special kind of charm. And he had selected me to spout his proclamations, being that I was the only other person in this corridor of Domodossola Station. From the tenor of his voice it was obvious, he didn't want a response. He wanted an audience.

He carried on about rights and freedoms while I had yet to utter a single word. My head was still reeling from the shock of his surprise attack on my solitude, not to mention his ongoing rant about our current state of affairs. Not that what he was saying seemed so wrong. It sounded like we shared some similar perspectives. Our world is a mess.

6

Suddenly it hit me. English? He's speaking English. Here? I don't look anything even close to your standard American traveler. In this remote border region, he'd be more likely to assume I spoke Italian, or French, or even German, but not English.

"My dear friend, don't you see? It is futile. We are powerless. Powerless against the forces that control our lives," he charged while stretching his long, boney fingers out to me. "Let a fellow sinner use your Bic."

I didn't realize it was still tightly grasped in my hand.

"My name is Silvio, your new friend. Or, should I say associate? Yes, your new associate," he decreed while reaching yet again, this time to shake my hand. "I always enjoy meeting Americans. You are so," he paused, clearing his throat to ensure his sarcasm was to be fully appreciated, "so delightfully *righteous*."

He smirked as we fumbled for a moment, shaking hands and passing the Bic back and forth. I also fumbled over his none too subtle attack on Americans. Being an avid international traveler I'm quite accustomed to the blunt outrage expressed by many around the world concerning America these days. However, I didn't have a need at the moment to defend, or explain, or deal with it. I smiled back, with my own version of a smirk.

The train shot out a high-pitched blast, the warning whistle for departure. Soon I would have peace and quiet, once again. I took a last long drag off my smoke before crushing it on the pavement among the collection of butts left by the other travelers who could no longer smoke on the trains in Italy.

"What's your rush, my friend?" He paused, rolled his steel-gray eyes. "That's right – the American. Always in a hurry."

My rush had nothing to do with being American; it had everything to do with escaping. Apparently, he wasn't the type to read cues from his audience. So, in an attempt to redirect our conversation to a less intense topic, I made comment about having read this is one of the most breathtaking train routes in all of Europe. Something I'd browsed in the café at Geneva's Cornavin Station earlier that morning. But, he wasn't a taker on my attempted detour.

"You Americans have hurried yourself to the point that you've lost the true magic of life. The *illuminazione*, that unadulterated sense of happiness in the moment. Instead, you have created for yourself a lifestyle that became more valuable to you than family, than friends, than sitting at a café to drink your coffee. No, you don't have time. You drive through the Starbucks on your way to the place where you spend most of your time and live your *lies* for money."

He stepped back, his hypnotic gaze focused intently on me. I could tell it was time for his *grand finale*.

"America has failed you. It has failed all of us! Your war has become the whole world's war. In your rush to judgment, or lack of judgment, you have created the war *they* have always secretly awaited. America's destiny."

His stare deepened as he raged on.

"Your Mr. President Bush, he and his comrades are merely players in the *challenge*. You see my friend – this is the time of kingdoms falling."

Of course my interest was tweaked. How could it not be? Come on, kingdoms falling! I have definite opinions, particularly on that subject. However, over the past few weeks some version or another of that debate had been played out at every turn. Politics, religion and *your Mr. Boosh* (as it is pronounced throughout other parts of the world). My saving grace, I could honestly say I did not vote for that man and don't agree with America's invasion of Iraq. That would calm many a testy critic.

At times, my views on this subject actually worked to my advantage. I noticed the Dutch to be particularly open in the workplace regarding their political evaluation of America. And it's not positive. I often wondered how my Republican friends and associates handle this event while doing business overseas.

So if I respond now, my much needed mountain escape will turn into a lengthy and passionate debate about something or other that ultimately I can do nothing about. I can't change the world. I mean, sure I help those in need in my community, and I support charities that impact the lives of people in every part of the world. Most Americans do. But what can I do when it comes to corporate ethics, global relations and political agendas? Considering the interplay of governments, corporations, international alliances, rebel groups, and religions, it's all a chaotic web spun from greed and attitudes of superiority, controlled by a select few!

Basically this guy is right. I am powerless.

"You my friend, you don't appear to be the typical American." His tone softened. "I'm sure we both have something to gain from that."

I stood there pondering if I'd just been complimented or kindly insulted. The second and final departure whistle shrieked through the corridor. Freedom at last, I quietly celebrated. With a tilt of my head I wished him *arrivederci* and politely stepped aside for *Beetlejuice* to pull himself onto the train ahead of me. I'm typically polite, but in this case my niceness had far more to do with a desire to make sure this guy wouldn't sit anywhere near me. Having just spent the past couple of weeks traveling among the crowds and general over-stimulation of Southeast Asia and India, I was more than ready for this relaxing train ride through the

Italian Alps. I wasn't about to let anyone *or anything* interrupt the peaceful journey awaiting me.

With my new associate seated safely seven rows away, I took a seat in the last row on the last car of the train. The perfect spot, nestled on one side by a luggage compartment and on the other, a panoramic view of serenity.

Alone.

I was content in my own little corner of the world.

# chapter two

The train was surprisingly empty, but the Domodossola-Camedo Line isn't on your typical tourist's list of the *1000 places to see before you die*. This isolated route traverses a mountain pass in Northern Italy's Province of Verbano-Cusio-Ossola, which fingers between two disjointed segments of Switzerland. The rails wind along the steep and narrow grades of the Alps, featuring spectacular views of the quaint villages and beautiful vistas hosted by the mountainous terrain.

Regardless of the splendor, this route adds several hours to the day's journey. I'd just arrived from New Delhi earlier in the morning, and the day had already become a fiasco fueled by jetlag and culture shock. Ultimately, I missed the 08:10 express train to Lugano.

I arrived at the station in plenty of time to purchase my ticket and grab a cappuccino. Only, I had not anticipated the chaos of Friday morning's rush hour insanity at Cornavin Station – all spoken in French. The worst part, I just don't get French! The *billet* attendant obviously didn't get me either, as she ticketed me on a series of local lines to my final destination, requiring five transfers! There was nothing she could do, as she had already printed the tickets. By the time I made my way to the head of the queue at customer service for an exchange, my express train option had left the station.

So I'll start my weekend retreat in Lugano a few hours later than anticipated. That's fine. At least they speak Italian in that region of Switzerland, a European language I can somewhat decipher.

I had left Port Columbus International Airport over three weeks earlier for a business trip that would take me to Amsterdam, London, Zurich, Dubai, Dhaka, New Deli, and now, Geneva. A whirlwind tour! The company I'd started several years earlier boomed and time had come to expand operations internationally. A dream assignment for a wanderer like me. I've always had an unquenchable thirst for travel; particularly to places where I don't speak the language. I've found I can trust my instinct and heightened sense of intuition when I don't have words to distract me. I'm so much more keenly aware of life's nuances when simply observing through my soul.

From the early planning stages for this trip, I had an odd sense about it. At the risk of sounding like a new age guru, it was actually much more than just an odd sense. I honestly felt the energy of the Universe leading me to this place and time. Over the past few years, I'd experienced an increased awareness of God's hand in my life; the presence of something from within. And in regards to this business trip, I believe the voice of God directed me.

This is Storm Team Chief Meteorologist, Jym Ganahl, with an NBC 4 Weather Alert. The thunderstorms that have been pounding Central Ohio over the past few hours are expected to intensify. A new line of nasty storms, bringing with them high winds and possible hail, will reach the metro area within a matter of minutes. The unique atmospheric conditions that exist this evening are producing a spectacular lightshow throughout Central Ohio. With the extraordinarily high amount of electrical activity we've seen associated with this front, I urge you to take immediate cover indoors. All of Central Ohio remains under a tornado warning in effect until 3:00 this morning. Stay tuned to NBC 4 Columbus for further updates on this weather event. We now return you to our regularly scheduled...

♫ ♫ *Who could it be now*
♫ ♫ *Who could i ...*

Hello.

"Hi baby. Whatcha doin'?"

Oh, hi girl. Just chillin' out. Takin' in the storm, smokin' a bowl and thinkin' about life. What an ugly Saturday night, huh. – You goin' out in this?

"Well, I was hoping to come over. It's the perfect night for a snuggle partner. You game?"

You know baby, I think I'm gonna hang out alone tonight. I'm just not feelin' it.

"I hear it in your voice. Are you still wrestling over that international deal? I don't want you to go."

Yeah, I don't know what to do. I'm thinkin' it's the right move. The connections are there! Man, India is primed for huge economic growth. And with the strengthening Euro, our pricing structure easily beats our European competitors. International expansion is the right move! – Sorry, didn't mean to get preachy, baby.

"I know, you're still bummed. I don't get the international business stuff, but I believe in you. I could come over there and, make you feel better."

Not bummed. Fed up! The way things have been goin' lately is botherin' the hell out of me. I've got no say, no support, no understanding. It's just no fun anymore. I know the best thing to do is just take the plunge and do the trip. But, I don't wanna add to the drama. I'm just sick and tired of all the shit.

"Baby, you gotta do something. It's eatin' you alive."

Wow! Did you see that one? I'm out on the balcony and a lightning bolt just shot right across the entire downtown skyline. Damn, that was beautiful! Are you looking outside?

"Sure am, some fireworks. You better get inside where it's safe."

Hell yeah, I know. I'm an easy target for God right now. *Cha*, that would simplify things. No, it's too beautiful a storm not to be outside takin' it in.

There's another one. Excellent!

"Loud, too. – So, whatcha gonna do?"

Tonight?

"No, the trip."

Hell, I don't know. I've gotta get a move on travel arrangements and business visas right away if I'm gonna do this thing. I'm just afraid it'll cause too much dissension. Maybe its best I forget about the whole damn idea. – Just keep smilin' and limpin' along doing business as usual.

"That's not your style, baby. You didn't get to where you are by goin' along with the crowd, *biatch*."

You're funny. I know. I'm just tired of it, girl. Sorry, guess I'm feelin' pissy tonight. I'll figure it out. – Hey, let me let ya' go. The rain's really comin' down now. I can barely hear a word you're sayin' – I'll call you tomorrow, ok?

"Don't be so hard on yourself, you hear me?"

I won't baby.

"Sure you don't want company tonight? I'd come through this shitty storm to spend the night next to you."

Ah, you're a sweetheart. No. Stay home where it's safe. I just wanna be alone tonight. You understand, right?

"Of course I do, baby."

Thanks girl. Well, hey - sweet dreams. Love ya'.

"Love you, too. We'll talk tomorrow. B'bye."

Oh, God. What the hell. Do you want to give me a hand with this one? I'm tired. I need something else, God. A new life. *Something.* So what do you say, God? – Hey, that was a loud one! And the lightning a little too close for comfort.

Please don't take me out just quite yet, Lord.

I'm not ready.

*That time has not yet come. And, no you are not!*

God?

*Do not be afraid, my child. Since the first day that you set your mind to gain understanding and to humble yourself before your God, your words were heard, and I have come in response to them.*

I hear you! I mean, I can actually *hear* you.

*Listen to my words. Follow the path I've placed before you. The steps you take will lead to many wonders and depth of insight.*

What path?

*Listen! The journey you are to take will be blessed. Follow the way love leads.*

Journey? You mean my business trip?

*Isn't that what you asked me about?*

Yeah, I guess I did. I really wasn't expecting an answer, though.

*Then why'd you ask?*

Maybe I just wanted to believe...

Is this really, *really* you God?

*Faith, I ask of you. The choice is yours, yet my way leads to peace, hope and joy.*

*Finally, never fail to remember.*

*I AM Love.*

❦

Hearing God's voice probably sounds a little *out there* to you. I agree. It does. But in my defense, a recent study led by Penny Edgell, Associate Professor of Sociology at the University of Minnesota, found that, "atheists, who account for about three percent of the U.S. population, offer a glaring exception to the rule of increasing social tolerance over the last 30 years." Given Professor Edgell's findings, not only am I part of the overwhelming majority of Americans who believe in a higher power, but apparently we Americans, as a whole, don't like people who don't believe.

Well, I've pretty much always had faith in God. To this day, some forty years later, I still have an amazingly clear recollection of *the hour I first believed*. I was only five years old when my spiritual epiphany, the awareness of the power that encircled me, guided me, and protected me, was miraculously revealed.

It was the summer of 1966. I attended a good ole fashioned Southern Baptist tent revival with my family, deep in the rolling hills of Southeastern Ohio. We drove into the Appalachian countryside to a place where cars lined both sides of a dusty gravel road. I recall the soft glow of lights shining from under the open air tent and the resonance of hymns lofting in the evening breeze.

It was one of those rare Ohio summer nights, not too hot and without the typical oppressive humidity. The only dampness in the air was the chill of evening dew, ushered in by the setting sun. A grove of pine trees surrounded us, sharing their sweet scent of Christmas. The full moon hung low in the summer sky, making it appear larger than life. I clearly recall standing there, my eyes and soul fully open, consumed by a sense of oneness.

As the hymns ended, the preacher walked to the front of the congregation and began to speak of God's love and salvation, all in a rich southern drawl. I was fixated to his every word. My heart began to pound as I listened, and I understood. Sure, I'd heard the stories before. But never had such life been breathed into the gospel. His words resounded in my mind, *love – a real, everlasting love.* I felt a tugging from within my being. My emotions began to stir. By the end of his sermon, I was shivering. It wasn't the chilly night air rolling into the valley that brought on my trembling. I knew what it was.

God's presence.

As those standing around me were singing the closing hymn, the pastor stepped forward, once again, and said, *"If the Lord is speaking to you, come. Jesus died for you and He is calling you to love as He has loved. We are all sinners and have fallen short of the Glory of God. Evil lurks in every corner of the universe. Ask Jesus to save you. He's the only atonement for evil. Will you heed His call?"*

The words of the hymn echoed in my head, as I battled my very young demons.

> *Amazing Grace, how sweet the sound,*
> *That saved a wretch like me.*
> *I once was lost but now am found,*
> *Was blind, but now, I see.*
>
> *T'was Grace that taught*
> *my heart to fear.*
> *And Grace, my fears relieved.*
> *How precious did that Grace appear,*
> *the hour I first believed.*

This man knew me. He knew God's Word was in my heart, calling out to me.

The preacher made a final plea, *"Will you trust Jesus Christ to be your Lord and Savior?"*

While many of those around me began to stream to the altar to answer *His* call, the feeling of being pulled, yet resisting, became overwhelming. I felt torn by rivaling forces, spiritual forces. Why was I fighting it? I understood the message. Still, that sickening struggle persisted within my soul.

It wasn't the *sin* thing that haunted me. Hell, the worst sin I had time to commit by the age of five was showing the neighbor girl my thing. (Come to think of it, that's a sin I've had an affinity for pretty much all my life.) Nor was it even the *eternal life* thing, although that seemed pretty cool. It was the *love – the real, everlasting love* thing. My struggle was with the charge to live and love like Jesus. I took the responsibility of that commandment to heart, and knew I couldn't do it.

As my internal battle persisted, out of complete frustration, I cried, *"God help me!"* What happened next makes little sense to the rational mind. However, an energy outside myself touched me. Lifting me to my feet, it carried me to the altar. Grace fell upon my soul. Standing there in front of God and everybody, I stared up at the pastor. The words, "I want to ask Jesus to come into my life," flowed from my lips.

At first glance, a look of bewilderment came over the pastor's face, as he gazed into the eyes of a child. Quickly recovering, he quoted the Bible with a gleaming smile. "Jesus said, *Let the little children come to me, and do not hinder them, for the kingdom of God belongs to such as these.*"

He then asked me to repeat to the congregation what I'd just said to him. I did. The beauty of that moment touched every soul under that tent. I remember people applauding, cheering, and even crying for me upon finishing my statement.

Apparently, I made the right decision.

My family and I were asked to stay after, as the pastor wanted to interrogate me about my faith and understanding. He expressed concern regarding the decision-making abilities of his new convert.

"But, I don't want us to *hinder* the boy."

He pulled me aside and after a 20 minute debriefing, which ended in prayer and a *laying on of hands*, reported back to my mom and dad. "That boy's got the *Holy Spirit* in him. I have never…"

That night, I received prophetic words. Words that have stayed with me through all my years.

"The Lord has chosen you at a very young age, my child. He definitely has a purpose for your life. Don't walk away."

Great. Just what I needed – the responsibility to save the world at the age of five.

As I was saying, God, the Universe, Destiny, the Creator, whatever you call Him, spoke to me about this business trip. And I'm glad I listened! Every imaginable break had come my way. Right off the jet, I closed a hard sell in Amsterdam. From there, every stop in Europe, the Middle East, Southeast Asia, and India seemed to turn into a deal. And it wasn't just the business connections. I was experiencing unbelievable people connections, too.

Have you ever had one of those days where you're in a miraculous fog of happiness? One of those extraordinary days where the world seems *right*. I love those days. They usually happen to me in the early spring or in the dead of winter. People seem friendlier on those early spring mornings when the birds are singing and the smell of fresh cut grass fills the air. When all the world is abloom. Yet standing alone on a snowy winter's morn, amidst the absolute silence of creation, fills me with a greater awareness of the awesomeness of our world.

Well, that was the kind of month I'd been having. The strangest things continually happened to me. Good things. The list was endless, but cool kept comin' my way. Things like being bumped to first class, twice, on international flights; or having stranger after stranger come up to me in bars, with our interaction always concluding with an insistence on buying my drinks. However, the strangest thing of all was the wave.

Strangers in airports, on the other side of storefronts, across parks and city streets – it didn't matter where I went, strangers would wave to me. I'm not saying once or twice. I'm saying several times a day. They would simply wave and smile, smile and wave. It was really beginning to freak me out. And I sure as hell wasn't about to share this phenomenon with anyone. They'd think I'd lost it! Regardless, this whole trip was magic. I was simply *hot* and makin' connections.

Yet, there was something else about this journey, something just beyond my comprehension. Similar to a thorn in my side. Or, maybe I brought some old thorn with me from the States. I had plenty. I wanted to leave them behind, but I just couldn't seem to escape their prick. And this thorn was actually becoming more irritating than my others. Just when I was celebrating the wonders of *being in the right place at the right time!*

I guess it hit me upon my arrival to Bangladesh. I'd just departed the Middle Eastern city of Dubai, UAE – the *new address* for global business. Hell, even Halliburton has moved their World Headquarters to Dubai; a paradise where the floors of the subways are covered in marble. Traveling directly from the wealth, opulence and grandeur of this magnificent city, to then find myself in Bangladesh, the reality of so many parts of our world struck me like a punch in the gut – *poverty*.

Bangladesh is one of the most underdeveloped, yet densely inhabited countries on the planet. Its primarily Muslim population of 147 million lives in a delta floodplain at the northernmost point of the Bay of Bengal on the Indian Ocean. The Bangladeshis survive on an annual per capita income roughly equal to that of one night's tips for a waiter working a decent New York City restaurant. Needless to say, poverty is an issue.

However, through ongoing domestic and international efforts, Bangladesh is seeing increased literacy rates, achieving greater equality in education and reducing the growth rate of its population. These efforts to improve the economic and demographic situation of the country are paying off. As a result, the business climate is improving in Bangladesh. One example is the textile industry. Look at the tag inside your shirt. Notice something? There's a good chance it was made in this striving country.

Dhaka, the country's capital, is home to nearly 12 million people and has the tempo of any major metropolitan area. Well, with the exception of an occasional ox stumbling down a congested city thoroughfare or that alcohol consumption is illegal.

I was the houseguest of one of the country's elite, a well traveled and educated businessman with the right pedigree. His multi-level apartment, adorned with modern art to accent its marble and granite interior, was situated within the fortifications of the diplomatic sector. The neighborhoods inside the compound were extremely well maintained, considering the lush vegetation, which is characteristic of the region. Each entrance was festooned with armed guards, manning their checkpoints, ensuring the safety of the many international guests under their watch.

I should have realized the need for caution when first stepping out of Dhaka-Zia International Airport. A clear indication was the bullet hole riddled billboard welcoming me to the country. Periodic uprisings are known to occur, which was the case on my visit. No harm done. I was told to cancel my meetings and stay home for the day, as it would be over by tomorrow. And it was. However, safety is always a concern when one stands out as much as I did. They made the distinction quite clear – there are brown people and there are white people. I was a white people, which brings with it varying degrees of fascination and distrust.

The beauty of this country is found in its wonderfully colorful people. The Bangladeshis are *simply kind*, a merging of dignity and humility. There's a true sense of brother and sisterhood among these people, seen in their every interaction. Confused by their closeness, I noted to my host how surprised I was by the number of openly homosexual men there were in Dhaka. I had seen numerous guys walking the streets holding hands. He smiled, as if this were not the first time he'd responded to such an observation. I soon learned that holding hands was quite common among the men, as they see each other as brothers. And I was assured that a Bangladeshi brother would die for his friend.

Now that's putting *love thy neighbor as thyself* into action.

The Bangladeshis treated me like a king. My host ensured my every wish was fulfilled. He had dinner parties in my honor with the rich and famous of Dhaka. And he showed me the way to the international club, the only place in town to *legally* drink.

I ended up spending several evenings at the IC, drinking Dutch beer followed by Irish whiskey, hanging with the ex-pats in town. They shared the joys of the international lifestyle and praised the ability to live like royalty in this country. With the ridiculously low cost of labor, there's really no need to attend to the mundane chores of life. One guy told me they have their garbage picked up from their doorstep each morning for what amounts to much less than a penny a day. This was followed by another's response, "The real benefit of that job is the *trashman* gets first dibs on whatever food may have been thrown out from last night's dinner." As I laughed along with my fellow members of the civilized world, that thorn in my side deepened.

There I was, in my Versace glasses wearing $250-a-pair Diesel jeans with the strategically placed tear on the upper left leg noticeably just below the tail of my un-tucked Ben Sherman vertically-striped shirt, laughing over the evil of our world – the suffering of others. Had I really become that calloused? No, it's just that these people were potential business opportunities. There wasn't a need to possibly threaten a future business relationship by making an issue of it. And why should I be the one to get all righteous about the plight of the Bangladeshi people?

Even in their desperation, I found a simple happiness in the eyes of the Bangladeshis. These hardworking people always seemed to be laughing and touching one another. What they possess, even through extreme hardship, is a precious concern for one another – a love that binds.

Maybe I had something more to gain from them, besides cheap labor.

For the remainder of my time in that region, I tried to block out the desperation of those whose paths I crossed. It was just too much to bear. I needed to stay focused on business. That's why I came. But, I could still see the eyes of the children of Bangladesh and India just outside the window of my chauffeured rides. As they would beg for survival, their big brown eyes pierced my heart. I thought I had finally escaped, settling into my first class seat departing Delhi for the western world. Strange, the only English magazine they had onboard was National Geographic, with a special report on Africa. It was then I realized there is no escaping the reality of my world.

The wheels speeding along the rails produced a symphonic masterpiece, dramatically supported by the rhythmic sway of the train cars snaking their way up the mountain pass. The enthralling beauty just outside my window was something one would only expect to see at a Walt Disney park. Simply magical.

I noticed the border agent had made his way to my car. I shuffled for my passport and ticket, being quite familiar with the drill. I hate it when they carry those little machine guns draped over their arm. It just makes me feel guilty! And this guy was doing a more than routine check of my passport. Some people look upon me with extreme skepticism, and he happened to be one of them. Or maybe it was just the blue passport I was carrying; more anti-American bullshit.

As I sat there, I began to reflect on all that had happened on this journey. I had to laugh, thinking what a long strange trip it had been. I knew I was truly blessed. All I pursued, I gained. In contrast, my life in the States had grown tiresome and this trip allowed me the time I needed to fully delve into my subconscious mind. I was away from the image, the pace and the demands of my daily routine, which had prevented any genuine form of self-evaluation. It was here, in the mountains of Italy, I could find the peace that had escaped me.

In many ways, I am an alien. At least that's what my friends would call me. A complex man, possessing the idealism of a teenager coupled with the wisdom of a seasoned psychologist. While being a hard driving bastard of a businessman, I would often surprise the casual observer by my random acts of kindness. This paradoxical approach to life was just my nature, and it helped keep me amused. Otherwise, life would be such a bore. I was not prone to accepting boredom in life. I wanted to live like a rock star and enjoy each new experience as it presented itself in my world. And I was pulling it off.

The events of the past weeks only strengthened my position of power and wealth. I was filled with self-confidence and possessed a pride that only comes to those who reach the top of their game. My game was on – professionally, socially and spiritually. Never in my life had I demanded such attention, particularly that of beautiful girls – the biggest payoff for my hard work. All the joys that money can buy, and there's a lot of joy out there to conquer.

On the other hand, I'm really not as shallow as I make it out to be. See, that's the problem of having two strong-willed sides to your being. At least in my case, the angel on my one shoulder had a louder voice than the little red dude hanging out on the other. And I lived it. I would often share my views on the powers of the Universe – good and evil. Thus, my dilemma. The spiritual world I so freely divulged to those around me required a commitment of sorts. I had always believed, *"From everyone who has been given much, much will be demanded; and from the one who has been entrusted with much, much more will be asked."* There was no doubt that I'd been given much. However, the expectations that accompanied it were becoming burdensome.

The train approached the first of many tunnels situated along this route. As sunlight gave way to the darkness and chill of that passageway, I could see my reflection in the blackened window. I looked into my own green eyes; the returning stare stirred my soul.

Those hungry brown eyes, just on the other side of the glass.

My wound deepened.

# chapter three

"My friend, come with me and I will share with you a secret."

I flinched at the sound of his voice, which released me from the dreamscape I'd been drifting through.

"Oh, I startled you. I must apologize."

The face was the same, but his manner was entirely different. He read my body language. His apology seemed sincere. From all appearances, Silvio was now a kinder, gentler *crazy person*.

"Come, come," he said with a smile and a wink, holding up an unlit cigarette. "We can smoke out here," he said with a whisper while directing me to the door located just behind my seat. "Now that the border agent has come through, we are free from here to eternity."

If it hadn't been that I was jonesin' for a smoke, I would've passed on his offer. I'd just opened the bottle I picked up back at the last station, and a smoke with my wine would be delightful. He did seem a little less abrasive now that we were en route. I poured a glass and headed to the egress to join him.

"I may have been a little too forward earlier, my friend. I hope you will forgive me," he said with the utmost sincerity. "I just get excited. It's the challenge! We are, as one might say, in a world of hurt." The corners of his mouth curled upward ever so slightly as he paused for a response.

I really wanted to ask him how he knew I was American. My assumption was that he'd overheard me while I was buying wine from the shop girl back at the last station. She was cute and I *had* to flirt. In English of course, throwing in a few Italian words I had learned for just such an occasion. She was a *bella*. I think she got the idea even without fully comprehending what I was saying. I got a big smile out of her, regardless. It had to have been there. But, what's with this *challenge* thing? That was the second time he'd used those words. – I'm not goin' there! I'll take a smoke break with the dude, but I'm not gonna help him solve the world's problems. Not today.

"You appear to be a man of wealth and taste," he interjected.

My hesitation worked. Finally an acceptable topic. I'm good with talkin' about *wealth and taste*. Sufficiently superficial.

"I know what I'm saying, I *know* people. You sir, you have it all. Like a gift. Free for the taking. Trust in me, there is much more to come."

I explained that I certainly do enjoy the finer things in life. Within reason, I thought to myself. I really wasn't *that* rich. Without the need for exaggeration, I told him the short version of my recent travels. Leaving out the depressing stuff and only briefly elaborated on my business successes. Stories of luxury hotels, fine restaurants, great wine, and beautiful women always makes for more interesting travelers' chit-chat. And he was right; I also believed there was much more to come my way.

"So what's *your* secret, my son?"

I must have looked a little puzzled by his question.

He continued, "I mean a young man like yourself, traveling the world and apparently closing some pretty lucrative deals with multi-nationals. Living the good life. You must be a very proud man."

For the first time since meeting Silvio, I began to disclose a little more of myself. He really didn't seem so crazy after all. In an odd way, I really liked this guy. His charisma was intoxicating. Or, maybe it was just his compliment about my being a *young man.* At most, he was only fifteen years my senior. I do look good for my age, though. *Yeah baby*, the guess my age contest. A game the girls love to play with me, and one that I have perfected. You only keep the upper hand so long as you don't unveil too many truths.

I knew the odds of ever seeing this guy again were pretty slim. I did need to get some things out of my head. So, relaxed by the wine, I began to share the intimate details of my emotional wanderings. I felt I had a mission in life; one that I couldn't walk away from. Part of me wanted to chuck the chores of daily life and commit myself to serving those in need, or spend my time offering my talents to a good cause. I was at a crossroads and needed to choose the right path. However, the good life has so many privileges and my opportunities for greater professional accomplishments kept mounting. Recently, everything I touched turned to gold. Maybe *that* was the sign I had been seeking.

Then there was my dream of escaping life and finding a nice little beach village to call home. I already knew just the place. Lavra,

Portugal, a fishing and farming village a few kilometers north of Porto. Or Oporto, as we Americans say it. I met a little angel from there, somewhere along the way. She made it sound so picturesque, so old-world. From the seclusion of Portugal it would be so much easier to block out what's happening in our world and live a truly simple life.

I really didn't know what to do, or maybe I was just being too deep and complicated about the whole situation. I was still fighting my demons. That was obvious. No worries, I'll patiently wait for the Universe to reveal the answer to my internal strife.

"Searching for your purpose is admirable, and your compassion is touching. However, you must never forget to love yourself first. That's the first rule of life. If you don't truly love yourself, you will never truly love another. You are too hard on yourself, my son. If you don't take care of *you* first, how in the world can you do anything to help those brown eyed children you keep gushing about?"

His point was well taken; I am too hard on myself. And I contribute to NGOs that do good works in the most desolate regions of our world. Silvio seemed to really get me. I'm typically the one who makes people feel comfortable enough to tell their dirty little secrets. But he was able to draw me out. He was telling me things that made sense, things I needed to hear. He just seemed to know things about me. It was almost uncanny. I actually stopped to consider, could it be that Silvio is the messenger announcing my purpose? Maybe God had arranged this meeting. Silvio didn't even bat an eye as I shared this thought with him.

"Hmm – God? Interesting you would mention that."

I'm a man in touch with the spiritual side of my personality, I explained, which has led me to believe the Universe directs our lives in some strange metaphysical way. Like this serendipitous meeting; in a few cigarettes' time, I had gained such salient insights. Silvio was one of those people whom once encountered thrusts you to a higher level of thinking. If you believe there is a God, you must believe He's not just sitting back taking it all in. The hand of God touches every aspect of our lives.

"You are very wise, my friend. Knowledge is power. Of course there's a spiritual side to our world, but it isn't the spirituality of your Religious Right! Nor is it the whimpering voices of those Christian pacifists trying to save the world. It's not even the God of our Muslim brothers." He stopped briefly to carefully choose his words. "You see, we must take things down to the *human* level. We are here to live out our destiny. Your path is already plotted, it's up to you to seek that path and trust that which, to use your words, *the Universe* places in your footsteps. *Carpe diem!*"

His encouragement hyped me like a shot of raw caffeine administered directly into my veins. I was pumped. I felt it too! I was destined for great things. Silvio was surely sent into my life by a spiritual force. The Universe had a message for me and I was ready to hear it, ready to seize the day!

"Think with this," he said while thumping his boney finger on my chest, "and *not* with this," pointing toward my forehead. "That, my friend, is the challenge you face. If you simply follow your heart, you will never be led astray. The heart is home to all our desires. Your *Universe* is going to offer you more than you have ever dreamed. That is, if you trust my words."

Again, I was a little spooked by my friend Beetlejuice. The person I met on the platform had returned. He had that look about him again. His magnetism waned as his fanatical rage re-engaged.

"Look at our world! It's in ruins. Crusaders from both régimes are engaged in a sacred battle. A war of the ages! Aren't *you* the admonisher of the *holy war*?"

He looked as if he had misspoken, like he'd slipped up – and he had. What the hell? I hadn't said one word about my views on any holy war. Any holy war anything! Where'd he pull that one out of? The problem is, on more than one occasion, I've shared my views regarding the current state of our world. I do believe we are living in the days of a holy war. But, he had no way of knowing that.

Absolutely no way!

"You think 9/11 was ghastly, just wait. September the 11th was a physical disaster orchestrated by arrogance. The next attack on America will be a *natural* disaster – the wrath of God! And just watch how your leaders handle that one. It says it all! God has turned his back on you, just as it was always meant to be. The time has come for America's last chapter, her final challenge."

I had to speak up in defense of my country; the people of America, not our political agenda. As a government, we are making enemies faster than we can kill them. However, as a people, we're the most giving in the world. Americans contribute more in the case of disaster relief than any other people in the world. God most certainly has not turned his back on us. We are a country founded on God. *In God We Trust!* Of course there are things, many things, that frustrate me about America and its corporate-political agendas. Still, it's the greatest nation in the world. There is evil everywhere. Not just in America!

"Our battle is fought, not with weapons of mass destruction, but within the soul. It's a battle that has been raging for eternity! If you are at war, you are a warrior. And you, my child, have been chosen to go to war. You think you already hold the truth, but you must wait. Soon you will see the light. Good and evil are very deceiving. There is no absolute good, no absolute evil. No absolute truth. If you want to save the world, you must first understand this enigma of our existence. Trust me."

Trust is something I never freely give. And at this point, I really didn't know what to believe, who to trust. Silvio had certainly gotten my mind racing, and I needed time to process all that had just bombarded its way into my world. My cigarette had long been out and I was more than ready to get back to soul searching, on my own.

I watched as Silvio completed his last puff and reached up to pull the butt from his lips. To my astonishment, he pinched the burning ember between his finger and thumb until extinguished, then smiled with the pride of an accomplished magician. The expression on my face must have been gratifying. He smirked, yet again. As we headed back into the main compartment, he stopped me for a parting thought.

"Oh, the secret. Don't you want to know *the secret?*"

I thought his secret had been we could get away with smoking on the trains in Italy. Obviously I was mistaken.

"Daniel, my secret is this. You see my son, to fully know God you must be like an alien. And you are most certainly an alien – with your antennas held high. To know God, you must have one antenna linked to Him, and the other aligned with the devil. If you don't fully know evil, you will never fully know God."

# chapter four

By this point, my relaxing mountain train ride had been derailed on its way to tranquility and headed straight to hell. See, there's good reason why we've always been taught to never discuss two things – politics or religion. And Silvio had sufficiently covered both topics in twenty minutes time. However, that wasn't the most disconcerting aspect of our conversation. It was his last statement, his *secret,* which really messed with my head. That riddle alone would baffle the best of us. But, my *name.* That was the blow that took me out.

My name is Daniel – my first name. Problem is, I go by my middle name. I always have. I'd never have introduced myself to him as *Daniel.* There are few places where that name ever comes up, like credit card transactions and airline travel.

But never socially.

Not only had he called me by my legal name, he also referred to me as an *alien*, the nickname I'd acquired back in Columbus. This man knew me, details about me, yet with no logical explanation as to how he could know. I'm a spiritual person, but I'm also a rational person. I believe the Universe speaks to us, but not while wearing an old t-shirt and in need of a shave!

Silvio scared me, yet intrigued me. Meeting him was like finding a monster in your bedroom closet. You want to run and hide, but have to take another look just to be sure it's really there. I'm not a lunatic! Something supernatural was taking place on this train. There was no place to run or hide; I couldn't if I tried. He was here for a reason and I was prepared to accept his message. I was ready to take another look into the closet and find my destiny, or my monster. I feared they may be one in the same.

So, what message am I to gain from this magical mystery tour? His words were direct, nevertheless confusing. They were clever, even counterintuitive. But that's what made it all so captivating. The *knowing God* thing – being in alliance with both God and the devil. It seems so wrong, but made sense once considered. My immediate reaction, *I don't want to know about evil.* However, perhaps these were the insights I had been lacking. Could it be? The more I know evil, the more my purpose will be revealed. Possibly, it's like knowing your enemy before going to battle.

I replayed his words over in my head.

> *We must take things down to the human level. We are all here to live out our destiny. Your path is already plotted, it is up to you to seek that path and trust that which the Universe places in your footsteps.*

I found myself trusting Silvio's words. How he knew the very nature of my soul really didn't matter. He just did, that was clear. What truly mattered, I take away from this spiritual convergence the knowledge necessary to fulfill my calling.

Then the excitement of the moment hit me. I was *chosen*; he made that clear. Chosen to hear the *voice* of the Universe. Chosen to hold the *knowledge* of the holy war; a battle fought not with physical weapons, but a war of souls. Yet, what about his anti-American sentiments? Could it be America has fallen from grace? Could his predictions be correct? Is America facing a natural disaster worse than 9/11? That's unimaginable! The excitement of my new found awareness dissipated as I considered the implications of such a disaster. Could it really be? Had God turned His back on us?

I found myself flipping from mania to trepidation recalling Silvio's pronouncements.

> *Good and evil are very deceiving. There is no absolute good, no absolute evil. No absolute truth. If you want to save the world, you must first understand this enigma of our existence.*

I needed to make sense of the enigma. I had to determine what questions to ask Silvio. I must absorb his spiritual wisdom before our time together ends. Aboard this train was a Master of Knowledge, from whom I could gain the enlightenment necessary to direct my destiny. But where do I begin to unravel the secrets of our universe?

Then it hit me. He had already given me the key. – I must think with my heart and put logic on hold. He assured, *"If you simply follow your heart, you will never be led astray."* I had to calm my mind to fully comprehend the challenge I faced. I reached for my bottle. I really should've picked up two for *this* journey. As I carefully poured that ruby red wine into my plastic glass, following the sway of the train car, I searched my heart for where to begin. The Alps outside my window had become a swash of colors racing past me. I was lost in my thoughts. The beauty around me was no longer of interest.

*Evil lives.* I repeated those words as a mantra, inducing a state of transcendental meditation. I must know evil to find my way. I must align with the devil to fully know God. I must let go of my old ways of thinking and permit myself to be used by the Universe.

I'd already sucked down my glass of wine; I really should've picked up more than one, dammit! Then the reality of his words hit me like a head rush. He'd already answered the question to my destiny. I didn't even catch it. – I am to go to war! I am a *spiritual warrior.*

Reality quickly made its way back into my thinking. What the hell? Am I nuts? Had I lost it? I'm a professional, highly educated man from the western world. Not a witch doctor living in the outback of some African nation. I needed to get things back into perspective. I needed to take a rational look at evil, and then make up my mind as to what in the world was happening on this train.

Evil is everywhere. Realizing this is the first step to gaining insight into our universe. I began delving into the evils that surround me. The first thing that came to mind was our current holy war. My frustration with the state of affairs in our world had haunted me for some time. Religion and nationalism had thrust our world into turmoil, into battles over God and Country, and oil. Church and State controversies are never simple to unravel. So that seemed like a logical place to start. I never back down from a good challenge.

I am proud to be an American, because of the people of America. But I'm far from proud of the political direction our nation has taken. I'm sure that's the consensus, whether you're Democrat or Republican. We are a nation divided. Look at the last two presidential elections. Both of which were pretty much 50/50 splits – with outcomes that are still a topic for debate. In such a political climate, no one is happy.

However, looking back on 9/11, we were a country united. Come to think of it, we had much of the world's sympathy and support in those days. And if there is such a thing as a *just war*, the attack in Afghanistan on Al-Qaeda and the Taliban was justifiable. The multi-national forces served the world well by freeing thousands from a terrorist state. As an example, the new freedoms afforded Afghani women speaks volumes to the success of that attack on evil.

But along the way, something else happened. We became prideful. Arrogant! We became a nation hearing a call to war – a war to rid the world of the *Axis of Evil.*

A world that is not ours to run.

I'm not convinced President Bush is truly an evil man, but rather a pawn in the shadow of evil's deception. I mean, look at his wife Laura. She's an absolute angel. And she stands proudly by his side. How much more pure a First Lady could we ask for, a librarian? However, there is one among his legion that I deeply fear. Evil has a way of masquerading itself in good intentions. I just think evil pride and corporate interests launched us into one really big, bad decision based on *facts* that were *evil lies*.

I've come to learn that evil lies always lead to disastrous consequences.

When then Secretary of State, General Colin Powell addressed the United Nations to present America's appeal for the invasion on Iraq, he was doing so with erroneous information held in his hand. On that day, he stood before all nations presenting the lies of a select few. I've always considered him the great hope of the Republican Party – a man of dignity, humility and honor. A man I could put my trust in as President of the United States. But that was not to be, as his fate was sealed on that dreadful day. He ended up being the whipping boy of our nation for someone else's deceit. Do you really believe it just so happened he's a black man?

In a recent interview published in *AARP The Magazine*, Mr. Powell said, "I'm sorry it happened and I wish those who *knew* better had spoken up at the time, but there isn't anything else I can say about it."

If he could say more, I wondered what it would be. General Powell always appeared to be a reluctant participant in that devilish scheme.

September 11, 2001 was the world's bleakest day. Millions around the globe, people from every nation, cried together. We shared a common experience on that day. We felt real pain for our brothers and sisters. Grief filled our hearts as we became one in spirit. One spirit, united against evil.

America received the prayers of the world in those days. Needless to say, we have long since lost the support we once humbly received from our neighbors.

Like I said, I'm a realist. I'm well aware that in some regions of the world, people were celebrating in the streets upon hearing the news – America was taken down to her knees. Thus, the beginning of the new holy war. That ghastly attack on humanity drew a line in the sand for each one of us – Muslim, Christian and Jew. It made every individual in every nation choose a side.

An allegiance.

Silvio's words invaded my thoughts. *"Good and evil are very deceiving. There is no absolute good, no absolute evil. No absolute truth."*

In the Arab and Muslim world, many believe the West will fall and Dubai will become the new New York, the new World's

Capital. When I was in Bangladesh, I had the opportunity at a dinner party to hear the Muslim perspective from the sons of the country's elite. Those twentysomethings convinced me that even *non-extremists* hold this belief. America was going to fall and the sins of a nation would be paid. *Calamity will fall upon the infidels,* one emphatically proclaimed. Even some of my international friends living in the States concede this view is quite common throughout other parts of the world.

Good and evil are very deceiving. Right and wrong is based on one's point of perspective! Our *axis of evil* considers us to be the *infidels*. Still, anyone who would kill innocent people for any cause seems pretty damn evil to me; regardless of whom the culprit. But in Iraq, we are proving them right. We have killed and maimed their people and our own. Death and hatred fill the streets of that bloody nation.

Rage filled my thoughts and boiled my blood as I considered the senseless deaths of our current tragedy. To make sense of this, I needed to view it from a human perspective, a personal perspective.

That's when my thoughts turned to Greg, a U.S. military soldier and a good friend. I'd just seen him a little over a month earlier while back in Ohio. He was home on leave from Iraq and we made time to get together for a kayaking trip. Greg had seen quite a bit of action over there and needed to get some things off his chest. Paddling down the scenic Hocking River was far better than any psychologist's couch, and I'm a good listener. He expressed the sadness, the struggles, the loneliness, and the strain that a war places on the warrior and his or her family.

Even through his anguish, Greg could share an encouraging perspective. He told me the realities of Iraq are not only what we see on the evening news. There are many Iraqis who are hopeful because of America's presence. He spoke of the children that would come up to him with smiles in their eyes, and the parents who had hope in theirs.

The bottom line for Greg was simple, "There are always two sides to everything. Regardless, I was called to serve my country."

That's what I like about Greg; he's open-minded, while still being faithful. When not fighting in Iraq, Greg works as a youth counselor for troubled inner-city kids. There's not an evil bone in his chiseled body. My time with Greg on that day prompted me to post the following words on my personal website.

*We may not agree with the war...*
*Still, we must ask God to bless and guide*
*the warrior.*

The church in America, however, leaves me wondering where God is in all of this. I've seen such ungodly behavior rooting out of His people. Where's the *love thy neighbor* and *turn the other cheek* in damning others? I've tried so many times to find a denomination that teaches what Jesus taught. But I honestly couldn't find one. They all seem hell bent on slamming whatever specific group they've identified as the enemy of their sect. The hunt for evildoers while lobbying Washington to ensure personal freedoms and responsibilities is given over to state supported morality laws.

Jesus wasn't a political prophet. He was a social radical that never *forced* anyone to believe in His Word. He taught to accept and care for one another, regardless of one's position. I sincerely question why the church feels that its place in today's society is to do exactly the opposite.

Have we really become a nation of self-righteous *dividers*? Come to think of it, we always have been. Sin and corruption fill the pulpits and pews of our nation's churches. Don't get me wrong, thank God they are there. Hopefully the truth will rub off. What pisses me off is when they cop the frickin' *holier than thou* attitude.

Reality is we've all fallen short. No one is perfect. If we call ourselves God's people, how then can we ignore the rights of those who are different than our clique? In Christ we are one. And one means one. Brothers and sisters in *Jesus!* When we ignore our brothers, we ignore God. Because we are one! Or, is that a part of the Word that can be dropped for convenience sake?

Division in the church must outrage God. Where in the Bible does it say to form separate groups based on what you think? God doesn't give a damn what *you* think! He's already spelled it out. We just aren't getting it. I overheard the pastor of a *white* country church I visited make a horrific racial slur right after his sermon on compassion. At least he waited until he was out of the sanctuary and in the parking lot of his little, misguided chapel. Hey, don't get me wrong. Racism is an equal opportunity employer. I was appalled when the usher of a *black* urban church told me that I probably wouldn't be comfortable there; I should check out a church where I would fit in. He ushered me out the door of God's house.

I'm tired of having to fit in!

"Judge not, that ye be not judged!" Isn't that pretty straight forward? But we don't do it. Usually a congregation can conceal their hate from outsiders. Well, except for one particular hatred. It's easy to find a church that damns homosexuals, right from the pulpit! How many of those who judge the sexual morality of others have lusted in their own heart? A sin is a sin, bro! – Like I'm gonna invite one of my gay or lesbian friends to church some Sunday morning. I'm sure that common attack on the evil of *their* sinful ways would certainly show the beauty of Christ's love.

*Let he who is without sin throw the first stone!*

This is the 21st century folks and these are God's people! Where is the love?

Ah, those churches probably don't want me as a member anyway.

As a society, we've lost our humility along with our humanity. *Exposure* has become central to the American way of life. We feed off the lives of others who are willing to have their deepest evils televised for pleasure, fame and fortune. We've raised a Godless generation where right and wrong can hardly be heard crying out from within their hearts. We have run God out of nearly every public place to ensure not one person's rights could possibly be infringed upon, while quietly stealing away every other personal freedom.

We now have a generation without moral truths to help filter the evils that surround them. For example, sex for recreation has swelled to new levels of popularity in America. Oral sex is common among our middle school aged kids; straight girls caress and kiss one another in the restrooms of bars; and the flamboyant promiscuity of our gay population has reached Roman proportions. Promiscuity among every group runs rampant and is dangerous, bringing with it the curse of disease and unwanted pregnancy. Casual sex breeds anger and hurt, and loss of dignity. It's somewhat like war on a personal level. The ultimate goal is the same – to conquer. Or, be conquered.

Sorry to sound all righteous, forgive me. My friends back in Columbus could certainly fill you in on some pretty steamy details about my life. I guess it's easier to see evil outside of one's self. Seeing inside is the challenge. We humans are so talented at finding fault. We blame our parents for screwing us up, we blame our co-workers for screwing things up, and we blame our spouses or kids or whoever for screwing our life up. We don't take responsibility for ourselves. We don't take responsibility for our actions. We're like animals, willing to attack with a vengeance those we once loved or called a friend. We're just a bunch of lawsuit-obsessed, soulless, road-raged fiends looking for our next dupe.

We knowingly hurt one another, and then attempt to negotiate deals with God. Only the problem is He's smarter than our *cognitive dissonance.* Thinking we can cheat, hate and lie, then cover it with good works is simply wrong. I wonder how many hours of community service is required to get one back in the good graces of God?

Maybe that's what Silvio meant when he said I must know evil; to know the evil living within me. Sad, but that one's easy. My anger is my evil, among a few indiscriminate others. I'm certainly no angel. But rage is the root of so much evil within each of us. Sure, I usually used my anger for a *just* cause. Nonetheless, the passion I held for love was only equaled by the force of my fury. I was tired of the indignation that fed my anger and the injustices of our world. I was fed up with it all. Why do I even give a shit? What difference would it make?

By this point, my bottle of wine was empty and I needed a smoke. I had made zero progress on my road to enlightenment. Just more questions to perplex me. The only thing that came from this little exercise in the examination of evil was that *evil lives.*

The train slowed as we approached the stop in a quiet mountain village to gather the awaiting passengers. I looked out the window to the station platform. Just on the other side of the glass, sitting there in full black garb, was a nun. I've always found a fascinating peacefulness in these women of God. Then again, I never attended parochial school. Their devotion and lifestyle of humility has always touched my heart. But this nun was different than most I've seen around the world. She was young and beautiful, with pure blue eyes. A dusting of freckles stretched out from her slightly turned up nose, while plumes of red hair escaped from under her slightly ajar habit. She looked angelic sitting there, all by herself, not ten meters away. Our eyes met which forced a smile from both of us, a warm and friendly non-verbal connection. For that brief moment, I thought to myself, our lives became as one.

Peace fell upon me.

I pondered what would lead such a beautiful girl to make such a dutiful lifestyle choice at such a youthful point in her years. Had she been emotionally scarred by some traumatic iniquity along the way? Or had she gained some extraordinary insight that led her to this place? Whether it was good or evil that brought her here, that smile told me she had found peace. No matter the reasons.

The train's whistle blast announced our return to locomotion. That little nun looked to me once again and waved as we pulled from the station.

# chapter five

"So, which way are you going, my friend?"

His timing was perfect. I needed to talk and I needed a smoke. I was glad, however, to begin our next conversation on less extreme matters. I responded to his question, explaining I was on my way to Lugano for a weekend holiday. Three days of doing nothing but devouring the local cuisine and having fun. I earned this break and was ready to enjoy it.

"Ah, *Paradiso* – the most seductively beautiful gem in the entire world." He paused for a moment, looking as if he had just rekindled some fond memory. "Three days is not nearly enough time for you to be consumed by paradise, unless we are willing to act fast."

I wasn't exactly sure what he was talking about, which was par for the course. He didn't give me a chance to question before commencing his lecture on the history and appeal of Lugano. I was well aware of much of what he was saying. I'm a Travel Channel addict and had recently seen an exposé on this extraordinary little city. After viewing that program, Lugano moved to the top of my list of destinations.

Lugano is a paradise, a community that combines Swiss efficiency with Italian elegance, in a setting of exceptional beauty. The rugged mountains of volcanic origin, which completely surrounded the city form *Lago di Lugano*, or Lake Lugano, the centerpiece of the valley. Lugano nestles around the mountainside, tracing the contour of rich blue waters. A lakeside promenade lined on both sides by lush, mature trees, create a canopy of shadows as one passes under their arch. This tranquil pathway journeys along the lake, complimented with gardens, fountains and works of modern art, from the old town shopping *distretto* to the district of Paradiso.

Located in the southern region of Switzerland, Lugano's popularity among well-to-dos and celebrities, along with its exquisite shopping, casinos and ignored prostitution, has earned it the nickname Monte Carlo of Switzerland. Dotted with palm trees and sidewalk cafés, this Mediterranean-style community is the largest town in the canton of Ticino, located less than 20 clicks from the border of Italy. Its 52,000 residents live and work along the inclines that overlook the fox-shaped lake below. Hosting wealth as well as beauty, this city is Switzerland's fourth largest banking center, home to over 100 international banking institutions.

Paradiso is where I'll drop my bags for the weekend. I was originally booked at the Hotel Dante Lugano. The Dante, a recently restored 19th Century hotel located in the heart of the old town, rests at the bottom of a funicular railway that drops down the mountainside from Lugano Station. It would've been an easy commute to my room. Now, I'll have to grab a taxi. Due to a booking date mix up, *with the sincerest of apologies*, I was bumped. Instead, I will be staying at the Holiday Inn Lugano. Not so luxurious, but who cares. I don't plan on staying in my room all that much. They do have a hotel bar, a definite priority in selecting one's accommodations.

"You will so enjoy your time in Lugano. It is a place with such allure that it has long been known as *Eden*."

I asked how he knew so much about Lugano. Silvio explained he'd conducted business there for years. Most recently, as a consultant with the Dalle Molle Institute for Artificial Intelligence at Università della Svizzera Italiana, a non-profit research institute for AI advancement.

"I was brought in as a consultant with their moral reasoning unit. You will find I know people in every walk of life, people you should know. My friend, what's your desire? What is it you want from your holiday in Eden? I can connect you with all the right people to make this a weekend you'll never forget."

Beginning to believe Silvio to be some kind of genie, I took his offer seriously. Besides, this wouldn't be the first time I'd gotten *hooked up* through a casual conversation on a train in Europe. Ok, this is no casual conversation, but you get the idea.

"Wait! Hold this," he commanded while passing me his cigarette. "I will make you an offer."

He bound through the doorway to where he'd been seated. I could see Silvio through the portal in the door as he reached up to retrieve a black backpack from the luggage rack hanging above his seat. He spun around and lunged down the aisle with definite purpose.

"Here. Is the backpack empty?"

He stood there pushing a Kipling backpack at me. I handed back his smoke and took the bag. I've always wanted a Kipling backpack, but was guessing that's not part of the deal. I like bags.

"You can't look inside," he quickly alerted. "Not quite yet."

The bag was empty from all appearances. I crushed it from every angle, fingered my way along its seams, and weighed it in the air. I assumed I was missing the ruse of his parable, but the bag was empty.

"Before you answer, don't you want to know the prize? If you give me the correct answer, anything you desire will be yours," he promised. "Be it fortune, woman, power, or fame. Actually, you can have it all!"

It was beginning to sound like I was here to make a deal with the devil. I figured it was in my best interest to avoid answering his allegory and wait to see where this would lead.

"Let me guess, your only weakness is women. My other offers didn't begin to turn your head. The only suitable enticement to tempt a man like you is the divine love of a woman."

I laughed, explaining he was right in a way. I had already experienced the bribes he offered, including the love of many women. But only one true love and that was long ago.

She was a flawless Lebanese angel. I may be exaggerating, but time has a way of glorifying its past. Her skin was a rich shade of olive, with the softness of a ripe peach just plucked from its branch. Her eyes, the shade of espresso – warm and deep. In her early 30s, she still spoke with a sweet innocence. Manar, an Arab name meaning guiding light, took on the nickname Claire while attending Catholic boarding high school in France. She was indeed a guiding light; the most charming and sophisticated little girl I have ever met. However, the best part, Claire was a playful imp when safe and secure in my arms.

She was a fashion magazine editor, with a direct demeanor while on the job. Regardless, her natural warmth would still shine through, assisting in the acceptance of her definite opinions. Claire split her time equally between Paris and New York, as she couldn't imagine living in just one place. A quirk carried since childhood. She was only twelve when the war broke out in her homeland. The rest of her childhood had been that of a wanderer, traveling with her family to their various residences around the globe.

I met Claire at a café near her brownstone in the West Village. It was Fashion Week in New York and she had been putting in long days and even longer nights. The previous night's parties had particularly taken their toll, so she slipped home for a power nap. Upon awaking to the rest of her day, she dropped in the café for a shot of espresso to kick her back into work mode. As she entered the café, our eyes immediately met, to never again separate. It was like magic. Truly one of those rare movie moments where two searching souls finally unite to capture a future filled with hope.

She missed a photo shoot and two interviews while we sat and discussed every intimate detail of our lives. The day turned into night as we walked the streets of Greenwich and questioned why it had taken so long to locate one another in this insane world. From that moment forward, the only thing that ever separated the two of us was work.

Our demanding careers only allowed us to see each other monthly, with an occasional surprise visit when I could no longer bear the loneliness. I remember Claire's reaction as the door of her Paris apartment would swing open and I emerged holding a single red rose. Her outburst of joy would simply make me melt. She'd call in, letting her people know she would be working from home for the day. My journey to heaven would commence. Claire truly knew me. She knew what I needed to be happy. And she would give just enough to keep me close.

Paris was her true love. Claire was more open, freer and somehow more at peace when she was there. When in New York, she had a difficult time even holding my hand in public. Paris was different. I remember the night I first realized this charming aberration. It was on a Paris train returning from the symphony. The car was packed and we were pushed to the front of the train. There, with hundreds of Parisians surrounding us, she passionately kissed me for at least two stops. That moment still warms my heart and stirs my senses.

Our life in Paris was beautiful. Her place was located in the heart of the Latin Quarter, one block from the *Sorbonne* and three from *l'Ecole Normale Superior*, the equivalent of Harvard and Oxford. This left bank neighborhood is the most intellectually stimulating district in all of Paris, possibly the entire world. We would regularly spend afternoons at a local café discussing art, world events, philosophy, and of course, fashion. She would translate for me when the conversation grew beyond just the two of us. Our evenings were usually spent at one of the neighborhood wine bars, the savvy *Le Mauzac* being our favorite.

Admittedly, our relationship was not always perfect. She definitely had two sides to her personality. Claire is a Gemini, by all means. There were those times where at a moment's notice her head would spin and the evil twin would arrive. In those instances, it was almost like she felt guilty for loving me, or she felt nothing for me at all. I knew it would only be temporary. Over the years I had become accustomed to patiently awaiting the return of her good sibling.

It was Christmas Eve. I had just arrived from JFK to Green Bay's Austin Straubel International Airport, via Cincinnati. Yeah, my miles are with Delta. That night's final destination, De Pere, Wisconsin – a small, red bricked town situated on both sides of the Fox River, where the rapids become unruly and the river runs north. Over the years, my family had migrated to this rare find of a town. Claire was insistent I spend Christmas with my mom. Christmas with the family would be wonderful, but I was already missing my love. Our extended holiday rendezvous in the City was sacred. We reached a new level of intimacy on that visit. She loved me with an erotic passion I had yet to experience in her arms.

Little did I know, it would be our last.

We had a thing. We'd text the moment either one would touch down in the next city. Our standard reply, *you make me melt.* But her reply didn't come. I checked the time. It was already 10:11 Central, 11:11 in the City. When I wasn't around, she preferred to prepare her tea and retire early. Still, she always had the phone by her side. That's just part of living far from the ones you love. However, the one I love was not available. After several texts and a couple calls, I was shaken. Of course the worst case scenarios were flashing through my head. She was relatively tall, yet petite in stature. I always worried about her when she was alone in the City.

By 4:30 a.m. Eastern, I was completely out of my head. She said she may run out for a quick bite at the Chinese place a few blocks over, if she got lonely for me. She always took the alley short-cut. I have preached the safety issue with her so many times. Her response was well rehearsed, "After living in Beirut, you learn not to fear." Claire was the type to stop and chat with the homeless guys. It's Christmas Eve. We have always fallen asleep while still talking on the phone, especially on our Christmas Eve's apart. Claire would always say, "It is so wonderful when I have you to share my sleep."

Out of complete desperation, I frantically redialed her obsessively. *"Not Christmas Eve. No Lord, please don't take her from me on the Eve of..."* Her voice finally came through from the other side.

"What are you doing? It's almost 5:00 in the morning!"

Claire had a way of reflecting blame when the other twin was making her presence known. I pleaded my case. I was so worried and *you always text back.*

"Well, Christmas Beirut time comes pretty damn early. I have phone calls to make!"

I knew her, more fully than anyone else. She always reminded me I was the only one whom she fully trusted. Then, it hit me. Hit me hard. I would have never imagined. I couldn't.

I shouted in agony, "Claire! You're not alone, are you?"

The phone went dead, as did my heart.

It was a general distaste for Americans, which resulted in an arranged marriage to a family friend that yanked her from my life. One day there, the next day gone. *Christmas Day.* The explanation I received came in the form of an email, informing me it was time she have children. Deep down, I always knew that no American blood would ever be permitted under the roof her father had provided.

She finally got in touch with me on February 14th of the New Year. How *totallyfuckingironic.* Her final words to me on that *lovely* international phone conversation were emotionless. "If you ever write a book, leave me out of it." – *Click!*

I'm a *frickin'* businessman! When the hell would I ever find the time to write a damn book?

Since that Christmas, the divine love of a woman was never permitted to consume my world. Denial and sophomoric hope will never again control me. Now I much prefer to keep the intimacy aspect of my relationships under my control, and at a distance. Well, except for the obvious.

Silvio made his observations. "I may not appear to be a romantic gentleman, but I do know love quite well. You, my son, you are one of the lucky ones. You were graced with the opportunity to experience the love of a lifetime, however short lived."

Again, he was right. I still cherish that moment, somewhere in time.

"I know this woman who lives just outside Lugano. You must meet her while you're in town. I believe she could be just your type – *the most amazing creation*. I'm sure she would find you to be a fascinating prospect. I must give you her number once we get back to our seats. Her name is Luna."

He had my attention. I would never pass on meeting an *amazing creation*. One must always remain hopeful, never missing an opportunity to enjoy the company of a beautiful woman. And that name, Luna, how incredibly enticing is that?

"So, the bag? Is it empty? Look me in the eyes and tell me what I long to hear."

Our *eyes* give us away. They reveal the gleaming light that shines from within our soul, if there is a light inside. Eyes can also lie for us; the source of the most believable kind of deception. I always seek that light in the eyes of those I encounter. Giving in to Silvio's questioning, I gave him the truth. I looked him in the eyes and said, the bag *appears* to be empty.

"You have learned nothing from our deliberations. You can't trick me. The bag is *not* empty!"

He seemed truly disillusioned with me, like I had failed him in some way.

"Let me guess, you intellectualized. Didn't you? You once again chose to use this," he sneered while pointing at my head. "Well, I must teach you to move beyond your world of criticism and judgment."

I think I do a pretty damn good job of not judging others. That has always been central to my personal values. However, I am one to critique every detail of a situation, intuitively. He was right, now that I look at it. I had analyzed good and evil with my intellect. Not my heart.

"Let me take this down to a practical level. Maybe your mind can grasp the literal," he smugly asserted. "Life is about each of us reaching our full potential. Our destiny. Self-actualization, that place where we actually become like God. To reach that level, you must learn to view the world through your passions. That which drives you from the heart. What is it that your heart desires?"

I began to answer, but Silvio must have decided he was better equipped to respond for me.

"You desire a new life, free from the lies of business and politics. Free, yet comfortable. In the blink of an eye, you would accept the kind of offer that would afford you the good life. Spending your time pursuing the creative passions you hold deeply inside. Art is the accomplice of love. And you need to be free from the expectations of this world to fervently experience love."

I have always been torn between the extremes of climbing the golden stairway of success and devoting myself to capturing love. For me, it had always been one way or the other. Except for the five years I shared with Claire. She made me a better man. That was the only time I ever truly felt balance in my life.

"So what's stopping you? What's your obstacle? I will tell you. It's quite simple. Fear. *Fear is evil!* It's what prevents you from cashing in on all life has to offer. You are hanging on to ancient fables of right and wrong. You still fear God. This is a new day, my friend. We are no longer hostages of the Law. God is not to be feared!"

He went on about those who had succeeded beyond their wildest dreams – business leaders, politicians, and the great artists and thinkers of the past. Those who did not fear God, but sought to possess all great knowledge. I remember as a child struggling with that concept – the fear of the Lord. I didn't like it, didn't agree with it. My God was a God of love and peace. A God that cares for the poor and the oppressed.

"Walk away from those ties that bind you. Be free to possess all that is rightfully yours. Remember, you are an alien. Make that link to both good and evil, and your life will never be the same."

His secret. I needed the answer to his mystical parable. I needed Silvio to hand me the wondrous key. The key to unlock the illusive enigma. I needed to know evil.

"That's what's been troubling you. Evil is the nature of the game. Can you give me one example where there is no evil in our world? Any decision made, any path taken, any life lived? No! Evil is part of our world and you must embrace it to gain the riches you so crave. You must be like a predator moving in on its prey. A thirst for more than just survival! A thirst for blood. Remember the first rule of *everything*? If you don't truly love yourself, you will never truly love. To fully love yourself, you must attain your destiny. Your full potential, no matter the cost. You will then be like God, holding all great knowledge and wisdom."

He gave me the key without my asking, but I found his references to God troublesome to my spirit. I know that loving one's self was the cornerstone of my success. I just have a hard time accepting that evil can be used to my advantage. I mean, I'm sure it can – but do I want it to?

"You see, my young apprentice, every single one of us has the devil inside. It's a matter of where you draw the line."

It was beginning to make sense, like a veil had been lifted. It's about *where I draw the line*. And just because I place myself before my neighbor doesn't mean I'm intentionally putting them down. I have rights too! Things I've worked hard to accomplish and possess. I will never let anyone take that away from me!

Yet, that line is *relative*. We manipulate our thoughts to justify our chosen perspectives. And at the heart of our perspectives, our selfish desires. That's why I must love myself above any other. Hell, they're doin' the same damn thing. It's a matter of self-preservation.

"You may wish to fight the injustices of this world, but you would be fighting from the wrong side if you don't put yourself first. Fully engage in the battle. Take your share and take no prisoners. Take what is yours. Live life on the edge, believing you are to acquire whatever is placed before you. Your gifts from the powers that be."

I realized not all the answers would be bestowed upon me during this short mountain train ride. For now, I was to gain the spiritual tools necessary to take a leap of faith whenever an opportunity arrives on my doorstep.

"Again, I ask you. Is the bag empty?"

I told my mentor I was sorry to disappoint, but could not honestly give him the correct answer. It was becoming clearer, but I was not yet ready to take that plunge.

"I assure you, you're progressing quite nicely. I'm thoroughly impressed with your inner synchronicity with the purely paradoxical principles of our existence. – What I mean to say is, you comprehend the depths of the old adage, *there are two sides to every story*."

His accolades were pleasing. I normally do not care to receive compliments from others. The result of my modesty, intertwined with a profound self-awareness of my strengths. I have never been one to need a hero to challenge me to greater heights. I've always done that for myself.

I was satisfied with the exchange of knowledge that took place. That's how it felt. Like Silvio had reached inside of me to plant a mystical seed. I could feel it sprouting in the pit of my stomach. Everything had changed within me. I was renewed. I felt hopeful and excited. I was beginning to grasp the secrets of the far reaches of my innermost being. That place just beyond comprehension.

"I'm excited for you to arrive in Lugano. You have come a long way for this opportunity, the opportunity to escape the challenges of your current life. You tell me of your passion for epicurean adventures and fine wine. I know just the place for you to dine this evening, *Ristorante al Portone*. An exclusive bastion of Nouvelle Italiana. A splendid grotto on the edge of the old town. Just your style. I know the proprietor, as luck would have it. His name is Damiano. Stop in tonight around 23:30 for dinner and drinks. Tell him Silvio recommended his curry, mango Chilean Sea Bass over sticky rice. An artistic creation that is so delectable it will poison your soul."

That may have been the best advice Silvio had shared all day. On one's first visit to a new city, finding a personally recommended dining experience is essential. And the *in* with the owner was perfect. At least I won't get ripped off like the typical American tourist. The Italians have a way with words, and money.

No wonder Rome ruled as long as it did.

"Remember my friend, no fear," he said glancing down at the backpack in his hand. "Always remember to draw the *line* to your advantage. I know people. I can help you."

We had both finished our last smoke for this installment of the Twilight Zone and headed back to the main compartment. I reminded him that I needed to get Luna's number. I wasn't about to miss this little charm of a gift. He walked to his seat and exchanged the backpack for a worn address book. Upon his return I was ready with my travel journal and pen to scribe his present. He flipped recklessly through the torn pages of his associates.

"Here we go. Give me your notebook."

Handing over my journal, I reflected on how remarkable an experience this chance meeting had been. More magic finding its way into my life, I smiled. As he scratched down her number, I expressed my sincere pleasure with our time together.

You know, Silvio, this is one of those rare moments in time where our *universe is magic*. Would you care to share your email? I would love to stay in touch.

I offered my business card in exchange.

Silvio flipped to a new page in my journal to write out his name and email. He looked up to me with a mischievous smile, apparently more than pleased with himself.

"My dear son, our universe *is* magic."

I took the journal from Silvio's hand and affixed my eyes to his email address… magic-universe@.

# 6Ô6

I was born a *Sunday's Child* on October 23$^{rd}$, the *day of creation* and dead in the center of the cusp between Libra and Scorpio.

What astrologers call *the day of conflicting karma.*

I am way too familiar with dancing atop that rope strung tightly between my opposing worlds. Life for me has always been a constant, living, breathing, ironic dichotomy. My search for balance had eluded me. It wasn't even a quest to champion constancy as much a struggle to fend off the conflict I've carried with me all my days.

The ability to see both sides of every situation.

Sure, having such a gift sounds like a blessing, but it's really a curse. I mean, think about it. How blessed is it, as a senior in high school, to fully empathize with the girlfriend who happens to be in the process of breaking up with you? It makes it really damn hard to get pissed at her. So, who takes the blame? Could it be, me?

I have always held the responsibility of others too closely to my chest. Don't ask me why. I don't feel I could be honest in answering you. But I do carry a cross for each and every person that has passed through my life. I remember you all, good and bad. The positive side, I can pretty much handle anything that slaps me across the face. Nothing shakes me. I pride myself on being a risk taker, living on the edge.

Experience has taught me to go for broke. I have always survived, and prospered. I had God on my side. I knew it. I knew because of freaky shit. Stuff has always happened to me. The "Kevin Bacon" kind of stuff. I remember a bumper sticker I had proudly posted on the back of my Subaru wagon in 1986 – *Shit Happens*. I had coined that phrase years earlier while a freshman at Ohio University, in another Athens. Yep, I was a psych major. It fit my attitude rightly – *that shit happens* and *no worries*. Then, years later, while living in the White Mountains of New Hampshire, I saw my pledge atop a rack at the corner market in North Conway. My sentiment had become a cultural philosophy. Bumper sticker wisdom! Pretty frickin' wild, huh?

As a student of psychology, I was instinctively drawn to the psychoanalytic school of thought. Of course Freud was a huge influence on my perspectives. However, upon resolving many repressed memories, Carl Jung, the renowned Swiss psychiatrist, became my idol. Jung's view of the unconscious mind more accurately aligned with my experiences and revelations. Freud saw the unconscious as little more than a repository for our repressed emotions and desires, a dumpster of disgust. Jung, on the other hand, saw it in a much more positive light. He contended the unconscious is also the harbor of one's creative abilities and home to our collective human psyche.

What Jung termed the *collective unconscious*, the governing dynamic that underlay the whole of human experience – *psychological, sociological, emotional, and spiritual,* held particular meaning in my life. His description of the collective unconscious as "a reservoir of the experiences of our species," validated my view of a unity among us all. I've always believed humanity to be interconnected by some spiritual force.

But it was Jung's concept of *synchronicity* that seized my intrigue. Jung believed that many experiences we perceive as coincidence are not due to chance, but rather suggest the manifestation of parallel events or circumstances. Events that happen, which at first appear to be a matter of chance, are later found to be causally related. Ever since my earliest memories, I've experienced synchronicity between my soul and our greater collective wisdom; some that I believe resonate with transcendental truth.

Ok, so I have to tell you what happened to me just a couple days earlier while in New Delhi. It helps explain the kind of *stuff* I've been talking about. – Synchronicity. But are there really any coincidences in life?

Having finished our five day business tour of Delhi, my new Indian collaborator, Gurinder, and I were out celebrating. He had selected *360°* in the Oberoi, a glorious hotel that harmoniously blends the tradition of Indian culture with the contemporary world of business. *360°* could easily be rated among the Top 100 restaurants in the world. Its postmodern minimalist décor contrasted appropriately with the world of poverty just outside its back door.

I met Gurinder via a buddy that lives in my building back in Columbus. Herb, a trendy and charming first generation Chinese-American, is a financial advisor who had made a name for himself by the age of 30. Now 40, he had left New York City to follow his physician wife to a new research opportunity with The Ohio State University Hospital. Her research had gone well, but their marriage didn't survive the transition from big city, east coast living to a Midwestern lifestyle. Herb was a good friend who could relate to my international tendencies, as he too had friends from around the globe. My Indian link, Gurinder, was another successful banker and drinking buddy of Herb's from their days in NYC. Upon the passing of his father, Gurinder graciously returned to India to manage the family business and care for his mother and sister. And he was bored.

My arrival on the scene had offered Gurinder new hope. The family transportation business was running itself and he needed a new challenge. A partnership with a U.S. company to serve the business needs of the rapidly growing Indian economy was just the move he was ready to make. Even more than hunger, enthusiasm drives the soul.

Gurinder's connections paid off. He and his American guest made quite a splash on the business scene in New Delhi. We actually had firms contacting us for presentations. It's that way in Delhi, all the elite know each other. If one does it, the others follow suit. Old money in young hands tends to promote such behaviors.

"Here's to a winning week and the start of a successful partnership," we toasted. Our intentions were to grab a table for dinner after a quick cocktail in the lounge. However, Gurinder knew the bartender who poured a mean Ketel One, Indian tonic with lemon. Besides, the lounge was more conducive to our boisterous celebratory conversation. We were on our second round of appetizers and third round of cocktails when I heard my name shouted out from across the bar. She hesitatingly questioned aloud, "Is that *you*?"

There we were, some ten-and-a-half time zones away from home, standing not ten feet away from one another. Reeling in shock, we puzzled over the astonishing odds and marveled over the millions of little boxes that fell into place for us to both be here, now.

Claudia and I had met on Match.com, and went out for dinner a couple times back in Columbus. Nothing serious, just plain enjoyment. She was a buyer for one of Les Wexner's brands, where she had accepted a position nine months earlier; an excellent career move, but one that uprooted her from the San Francisco lifestyle she so adored. She, too, was finishing up a week of business adventures and would be leaving the next day. Claudia was a guest at the Hyatt, which is quite a ways across town, but had been invited to dine at *360°* with the managing director of the textile group she was in to call on. *360°* is that kind of place, to impress and commemorate one's successes.

We made introductions as Claudia's host abruptly excused himself for the evening. Once he was barely a meter away, Claudia thanked me incessantly for saving her. Turns out, she was more than a little nervous. That rich prick's advances had gone way beyond any society's standard for professional or *social* behavior. She was honestly terrified.

It's fascinating how things seem to work out sometimes – and sad how they don't at others.

The three of us chatted away in the glow of this totally mind-blowing coincidence, which had shaken our perspectives of reality. What are the chances? They laughed about their new good luck charm, me, and the way the Universe had brought us all together.

Gurinder was truly amazed, "So, this sort of shit happens to you all the time? It must be emotionally exhausting."

By this time, it was getting late and we were not about to let a blonde haired, blue eyed cutie take another chance, this time with the integrity of some taxi driver. So the three of us decided to finish out our evening at the Italian bistro in Claudia's hotel. Once there, time allowed for two bottles of wine and plenty of lively conversation. Coincidence has a way of giving an evening flight. It also brought out a different side of Claudia.

In Columbus, she seemed so guarded, almost mechanical. The magic of that evening exposed her soft and sensitive side. The closeness we unexpectedly shared that night allowed Claudia to expose the most intimate details of her life. Her innermost secrets were laid on the table for the hands of relative strangers to touch. She appeared to be more real, more comfortable, more appealing.

It was way past closing time, so the manager ushered us out of his establishment. We stood on the steps just outside his bistro, discussing our next move. Probably off to raid Claudia's minibar. Suddenly, the voices of Americans, a man and woman, filled the empty granite corridor of the Hyatt's grand hallway, "Gurinder, is that *you?*"

I'm not making this shit up! It's just too damn incredible for fiction. Turns out, these two were business associates from Gurinder's days in the States. They had lost track of him when he relocated back to India. The couple was on their way to Bangalore for meetings, but due to flight delays followed by confusion at customs, they ended up in New Delhi for the night.

Now the three had become five, all living in some bizarre dimension of space and time. Happening once could be rationalized, but twice is definitely a miracle. We ended up sitting around Claudia's room until the minibar had been sufficiently ravaged and we were sufficiently wasted. Our conversation centered on God and the amazing events in this world that science will never be able to explain.

That's the kind of thing that calls for a *shit happens*. You know there's magic in the moment, but could never fully comprehend why. For me, why is no longer an issue.

What's next is where I focus my awareness.

So what's occurred since boarding this train doesn't catch me off guard in the least. Still, it is by far the most chilling example of the funky synchronicity that winds its way into my world. Yet, my enthusiasm was quickly starting to fade. Silvio seems to have an unspeakable power over me when in his presence. Once separated, the attraction lessened.

Starting our descent, the train was eerily silent, gliding down the winding path. It's extraordinary to be in the center of God's creation with no distraction from His grandeur. That void offered me a sense of clarity, as the sound of church bells began ringing from the valleys below. Each with its unique chime, and some minutes behind Greenwich Mean Time. Four in the afternoon, or so, and the saintly melody of those sanctuaries echoed throughout the countryside. That's one of the simple pleasures I gain from my time in Europe – the blessed song of the cathedral bells.

A sense of relaxation filtered through my body and soul. A feeling of enlightened peacefulness shone upon me. As the bells cried out, my heart ached. The beauty, not the beauty of the valley filled with church steeples, but the beauty of God. The ringing in my head softly transformed into the voices of angels singing. Over recent months, I had been experiencing God more abundantly. But today, God seemed more real to me than He had in such a long time.

My ongoing sensory overload, combined with that bottle of red wine, led me to a state of emotional mayhem. Delusions invaded my short-lived peace with an unanticipated anguish. I needed to just take a deep breath and chill. I tried. Yet, my emotions twisted inside out.

Tears began to stream down my face. Was it God's presence or the thought of Claire? That damn lump sitting squarely in my throat persisted. I had not permitted myself to think of her for so long. Occasionally she would awaken me from my dreams, but it's so easy to suppress those late night visitors who invade our sleep. I thought of our nights in Paris. She was an angel living in my soul. Had I ever fully regained my independence from her touch?

Suddenly all the emotions, and experiences, and successes, and too, the failures of my life rushed me simultaneously. It was like replaying my every step on this planet in fast forward. I saw visions of people I had not thought of for ages. The faces of those whose lives I had impacted, with good or evil. There, too, were the people who made an impression on my existence. And those who sinned against me, they were also exposed.

In that moment of insight, the truths of my life were revealed to me. No amount of money could buy this kind of psychoanalytic regression therapy. I really wasn't prepared to go down this path. And, *why now?* The muscles across my shoulders tightened like clinched jaws. I had never experienced vertigo, until now. This wasn't a panic attack. I don't panic. So, what the... That's it. It must be. Pixy dust. It's the frickin' pixy dust swirling around my head. I was reeling toward madness. Dr. Freud would have just loved this moment.

You know, life is so much easier when you have kids to attend to, and tee times to make, and drinks after work with associates. It's cleaner that way. Nice little frickin' boxes for everything and everyone. The right *crowd*, the right *clothes,* the right *car* and the right business *lines*. Those damn lines. Whooah!!!

My thoughts were way beyond manic. I've never had a nervous breakdown; however this experience was real damn close. This wasn't your ordinary internal conflict to be reckoned with; I was in the midst of a full-blown life crisis.

But why? Nothing was *really* wrong.

I pulled out my travel journal to study Silvio's email address and handwriting. I didn't really think I'd find answers there, but I needed to start somewhere. Just one more oddity, I thought while considering my prophetic statement, *our universe is magic.* His words were tempting and his offers appealing, but they were all too damn frightening. Looking at the journal in my hands, I decided to jot down the parables Silvio had presented.

We must take things down to the human level. We are all here to live out our destiny. Your path is already plotted, it is up to you to seek that path and trust that which the universe places in your footsteps.

Think with your heart, not your head. That is the challenge you face. If you simply follow your heart, you will never be led astray. The heart is the home to all our desires.

Our battle is fought, not with weapons of mass destruction, but within the soul. It's a battle that has been raging for eternity!

If you are at war, you are a warrior.

Good and evil are very deceiving. There is no absolute good, no absolute evil. No absolute truth.

To fully know God you must be like an alien. You must have one antenna connected to God and the other tied to the devil. If you don't fully know evil, you will never fully know God.

Life is about each of us reaching our full potential. Our destiny. Self-actualization is that place where we actually become like God.

*To reach that level, you must learn to view the world through your passions — that which drives you from the heart.*

*We are no longer hostages of the Law. God is not to be feared!*

*To fully love yourself, you must attain your destiny. You will then be like God — holding all great knowledge and wisdom.*

*Every one of us has the devil inside. It's a matter of where we draw the line.*

*Live life on the edge, believing that you are to take whatever is placed before you. Your gifts from the powers that be.*

*You must never forget to love yourself first.*

Well, now. That really didn't help. The list only offered more contradictions for my mind to dissect. Each statement seemed to hold a seed of truth, but often buried in a spoil of lies. Or so I thought. Silvio's words echoed hollowly through the core of my bones, *God is not to be feared.*

I always travel with two items – a Bible and a Saint Christopher's Medal. I'm not Catholic, but Claire had given me that somewhat tarnished souvenir. She received it from her grandma the day the family left Beirut. The fighting had increased and the war looked to be a long road ahead for the people of Lebanon. Her grandma was too ill to travel and stayed behind. That was the last time Claire saw that special angel she so dearly loved. Grandma was killed in a bombing raid, which mistakenly hit the family compound the very next day.

What are the odds?

That medal means a lot to me. I keep it tucked away in a small zippered compartment of my backpack. I never really pull it out and handle it. I guess the only time I'd do that is if I were on a jet that was falling from the sky, which is ironic. That would likely mean that ole Saint Christopher ultimately didn't do his job.

The Bible was a gift from Debbie, the sister of my best buddy from college. Michael, or Mikey as I prefer to call him, invited her down to O.U. for Little Sibs Weekend. We really hit it off, and she was absolutely beautiful. But making a move on my best buddy's little sis didn't seem fair. So instead, we ended up talking about God all night. It felt as if she thought my actions didn't really match my words. Deb encouraged me to read the Bible, every day. As she presented me with that little red book, she said, "It's so awesome how God will speak to you when you're in His Word. The Word is the place you will find the answers you seek."

Given the theme of this train ride, I gathered it was probably a real good time to retrieve that book from the bottom of my backpack. I play this game with God. I flip through the pages and randomly stop, taking in the verse my eyes settle on. I figure if God is going to speak to me, it's better for Him to take the lead.

Recklessly, I fingered through the passages until stopping atop page 434 – Psalm 34.

I silently prayed as I read His Word.

> [1] I will extol the LORD at all times;
>   his praise will always be on my lips.
> [2] My soul will boast in the LORD;
>   let the afflicted hear and rejoice.
> [3] Glorify the LORD with me;
>   let us exalt his name together.
>
> [4] I sought the LORD, and he answered me;
>   he delivered me from all my fears.

<sup>5</sup> Those who look to him are radiant;
their faces are never covered with shame.
<sup>6</sup> This poor man called, and the LORD heard him;
he saved him out of all his troubles.

<sup>7</sup> The angel of the LORD encamps around
those who fear him, and he delivers them.
<sup>8</sup> Taste and see that the LORD is good;
blessed is the man who takes refuge in him.

<sup>9</sup> Fear the LORD, you his saints,
for those who fear him lack nothing.
<sup>10</sup> The lions may grow weak and hungry,
but those who seek the LORD lack no good thing.

<sup>11</sup> Come, my children, listen to me;
I will teach you the fear of the LORD.

<sup>12</sup> Whoever of you loves life
and desires to see many good days,
<sup>13</sup> keep your tongue from evil
and your lips from speaking lies.

<sup>14</sup> Turn from evil and do good;
seek peace and pursue it.

Turn from evil and do good! Seek peace and pursue it! Pretty damn black and white, wouldn't you say? No, I really wasn't surprised. Debbie was right; God has a way of speaking to us if we simply take the time to listen.

Thinking of Deb, my mind drifted back to the days of Ohio U. Those were my glory days, the days before we'd heard of AIDS. The early 80s were a different planet in time. The B-52's, the Ramones and *Turning Japanese*. Oh, and *Baby's Got Blue Eyes*. That song always reminds me of my college love. She was the girl

I should've never let go. Life would have been so much simpler, so much more loving. A real, everlasting kind of love. Ah, but look at all the fun I would've missed!

I recalled the early spring Saturdays out at Stroud's Run, just over the ridge from Athens. Still too early for swimming, however perfect weather for beers and puff on the lakeshore. Our Rites of Spring. Those celebrations ringing in the season of the sun would include me, Bri, Mikey and Peters, each accompanied by the flavor of the week. Well, except for Bri. He and Anne have always been a team. Looking at it from this point in life, Brian's blessed. He's only had one true love.

Back in Athens, another sign of the season was the Spring Riot. The riots were an annual event left over from the Viet Nam Era of the early 1970s. Now, the affair is little more than a reason to party. Each spring, on the night we turn our clocks ahead one hour, Court Street in Athens fills with rowdy partiers streaming from the bars. Already pissed over being forced from their beers an hour early, they prepare for a celebratory confrontation with the Athens PD. The battles were much more subdued in the 80s, nothing like 1970. We no longer had a real cause to fight for. Nowadays, it was just a party with a purpose of destruction.

It was always a good time. A little living legend in A-town. The Post, O.U.'s student newspaper, would run the obligatory article warning of the latest police actions to curtail the event's impact on the city's streets. The headline read, *You Will Go to Jail, If...*, providing a full rundown of the various offenses punishable by jail time and hefty fines. But on page two started a lengthy photojournalistic recount glorifying the riots of days gone by.

The Viet Nam War was deadly and the U.S.A. was simply losing. And, losing the support of the American people. Much like Iraq is today. Students on every college campus across our nation were united, much *unlike* it is today. They believed in something enough to speak out and be heard. They were revolutionaries prepared to fight for their cause without fear of punishment. I joined their ranks back in the day, proudly wearing my peace sign necklace. I was only nine, so it helped that my mom encouraged such sentiments. She bought me the coolest tie-dyed shirts and let me grow my hair long. We'd relocated to Ohio from Southern California in the dawning of the *Summer of Love*. Thus the origin of my radical roots.

I liked being a hippie.

However, a repulsive message was bestowed upon our nation in those days. The pinnacle of our government's sins was reached on May 4, 1970 at Kent State University, a small liberal arts college in Northeastern Ohio. It hit me close to home, in many ways. Kent is located barely a two hour drive from my hometown of Nelsonville. I was young and impressionable, and my government had let me down.

May4.org summarizes the events leading to this tragedy. Pay particular attention to Nixon's "*not for the purpose of expanding the war*" comment. Please Mr. President; heed this warning calling out from the grave.

> On April 30th, President Nixon announced on national television that a massive American-South Vietnamese troop offensive into Cambodia was in progress. "We take these actions," Nixon said, "not for the purpose of expanding the war into Cambodia, but for the purpose of ending the war in Vietnam, and winning the just peace we all desire."

> These were familiar words to a war-weary public. Some felt that this decision was essential for attaining a "just peace" and sustaining America's credibility in the world. Yet others, particularly students, believed that this action represented an escalation of the war and a return

74

to ex-President Johnson's earlier hopes for a military victory.

As the fires from the artillery began to burn in Cambodia, a raging fire of protest spread across the United States.

On that day in May, the Ohio National Guard opened fire on a college green filled with 18-22 year old kids demonstrating an evil war. In 13 seconds time the Guard had fired 67 shots, wounding nine and killing four. I wonder what stopped them from taking out the whole damn crowd. I mean seriously? Did it really take 13 seconds for their moral compasses to become aligned?

Evil was there on that dreadful day.

The exact words used by that Ohio National Guard commander, standing there in the heartland of America, were "RIGHT HERE, GET SET, POINT, FIRE!"

A government should never find cause to attack its own people. If the government reaches a point where the people's voice and the political agenda are that far in contradiction, it is time for the government to rethink its position. Doing otherwise is just plain evil.

Here we are, decades later, a nation repeating the same mistakes. Every time I hear Crosby, Stills, Nash & Young's *Four Dead in Ohio*, my heart cries out for our nation's transgressions. It's now apparent we've learned nothing from Viet Nam. The only difference today is that we are no longer a society willing to stand up for a just cause. That would simply interfere with our lives – and livelihood.

Sorry, I got sidetracked. Ohio U. was an amazing place to attend for an education – a very diverse education. I liked it so much I earned three degrees from the *Harvard on the Hocking*. And

Debbie's Bible became a comfort to me throughout those days while struggling with my passage to independence. I even joined the Christian Student Fellowship that met each Sunday morning in Jeff Hall Library. We called him Steve, but Pastor Seevers probably has no idea how much of an impact he made on my life. I was so in tune with God back then. Not saying I was perfect or anything. I did use my Christian *Get Out of Jail Free* Card quite religiously. How cool is that! Jesus, the only Savior who gives us a loop-hole to sin. Grace!

That God of mine is so cool!

I hadn't pored over those memories in such a long time. I wonder how Deb's doing. I haven't asked Mikey about her in some time. Celebrating life, I'm sure. She has always lived the words she proclaimed. If you met her, you would witness one who truly has been blessed with the ability to reflect God's face. She just shines love. Her husband, the pastor of a dynamic North Carolina church, launched a non-profit focused on providing clean drinking water to villages in Africa. Very cool stuff. Check out what he's up to – www.zaowater.com.

Seriously, take a good look at the issue here. On the Zāo site they quote the following findings from the World Health Organization and UNICEF:

> In 2004, 2.2 million deaths worldwide were attributed to unsafe water; nine out of ten of these were children under five years of age. The lack of clean water kills an estimated **4,500 children a day**.

So much for *the least of these*. And while we are all busy worrying about oil, the day will soon come when water, not oil, will be the principal *re*source of conflict in our world.

There is one memory from those days at O.U. that has particularly impacted my belief system. It by far tops the list of my Ten Most

God Inspired Moments. It happened on a damp and chilly October's eve. I had gone to mom's for a quick visit, a home-cooked meal and to trade out the week's laundry. Thankfully she lived close enough that I could avoid the chore of laundry a little longer. I noticed the clock had moved more quickly than I realized, distracted by some intriguing mom-like conversation. Mom and I have always had a really honest relationship. Growing up together does that for you.

I had a Bible study to attend at the Student Union, and a date with a new girl at Toni's Pub afterwards. The perfect night. But, I was running late and needed to book. I knew exactly how long it would take, as I had traveled the road to Athens for many years. The good old, days when a sixteen year old kid could drink in the bars of Athens. Getting home was always an adventure. Singing *Dreamer,* by Supertramp, at the top of my lungs, while negotiating the curves of those rural roads. It was like flying.

Yes, I perfected one-eyed driving at a young age. It's a miracle I lived through those days of drunk driving the dark roads of Athens County. God, I pray my kids don't ever have a need to learn that desperate driving technique.

As I headed down Route 33, the moon hung directly in front of me. Full and bright, it fought its way through the clouds. I love autumn, and that night was a glorious example of God's handiwork. The clouds drifted rapidly before my eyes. My window was down and the misty air rushed my face, lofting the musky scent of tender bleeding leaves that too soon would turn to dust. It was then I heard God speak to me. It was a simple request. Perhaps too simple. I do tend to have quite the imagination. Possibly, it was just me playing God in my head. Yet it felt real.

God told me to take a turn. That's it. Just take a turn. He instructed me to take the exit at The Plains, a back way into Athens that rolls through the foothills that surround that gem of a community. The only problem, I was running late. Had I not been in a hurry, I would have followed God's request without question. What's more important? Getting to my Bible study on time or chasing some crazy mission from within? But my imagination wouldn't let up. As the exit drew near, an impending sense of oneness came over me. With it was pressure – *responsibility*. I had to do it. It was as if I had no other choice. I *had* to take the exit.

By the time I made my way over those winding roads and arrived at the edge of Athens, the clouds had turned black. The moon was now fully engulfed in a soupy murk of dampness. And I came all this way for nothing, I grimaced. Nothing happened, no great prophesy to share. Nothing.

I pulled to the intersection marked by a washed-out "Welcome to Athens" sign. Frustrated and late, I plotted my route uptown. It was then my headlights revealed a lone stranger standing along the roadside. I've never been one to pick up hitchhikers, but that sense came over me once again. I had to stop, regardless of my fears.

Maybe it was the fact that Halloween was near, or that I'd always carried a deep-seated fear of monster-like demons accosting me on those back roads I so frequently tread. But the thought of stopping on this dreary October's eve to pick up some crazed psycho killer was not my idea of fun. Evil lurks in these hills. Really. Google "ghosts of Athens" and you'll see.

My car barely came to a complete stop when the passenger door swung open and a gust of autumn haze filled my car. The stranger appeared from the dark of night. In his thick Appalachian accent he yelled, "Praise the Lord!" He settled into his seat and reached for the safety belt. Just then, the sky opened wide and let loose with a torrential downpour.

Occasional flashes of lightning would allow for a brief glimpse of the road ahead. As my wiper blades fought off the sheets of rain the stranger told me that I was a *Godsend.* His car had broken down several miles back and he had been praying for a ride. I asked where he needed to go. His destination, a country church on the other side of town. He was late for a Bible study. I told him I could relate.

Needless to say, we were both elated by the wondrous hand of God so near to us. We even prayed together before I dropped him off. How beautiful an Act of God to share with our Bible groups that evening. His was Pentecostal, so I figured their show of joy to the Lord was a little more animated than the group to which I belonged.

That was the moment God showed me He really does speak to us, and answers prayers. A cornerstone of who I am today. I never have a need to question His existence. As Albert Einstein once said, *"There are only two ways to live your life. One is as though nothing is a miracle. The other is as though everything is a miracle."* I live my life within the realm of the latter.

The blast of the train's whistle shook me from my mental dissection as we approached a charming cobblestone station. I questioned where the hell these memories had come from? Regardless, my session with Dr. Freud had proceeded rather nicely. This little lifetime regression is probably a healthy exercise for my mind and soul. Then a realization struck me from out of the blue. I was actually searching for something specific; some grand insight into my current situation. Something inside of me, deeply repressed. *Boots* would have been the obvious, but that wasn't it. There was something much deeper.

Boots. I hadn't thought about him in a hell of a long time. He was a good friend back in the day. I actually got in huge trouble for a paper I wrote about him. It was an eighth grade creative writing assignment. Mrs. Wolfe was nearly pushed off the deep end with my story. It was huge! I was tossed out of class, the school district's social worker was called in and my mom and dad ended up raising hell for my rights.

It all started when I was called to the head of the class to read my paper. I've always hated reading out loud. Back then, dyslexia had yet to be diagnosed. Mrs. Wolfe and I just didn't see eye-to-eye. She was an English teacher who preferred sentence diagramming. I was more the *do it by feel* kind of kid.

Anyway, upon completing my reading, which was actually a memorized recitation practiced over and over in front of the bathroom mirror for this nerve racking event, everyone raved. Even Mrs. Wolfe. I got the gold star for the day. I was proud. It felt good to have my friends, and Mrs. Wolfe, like my story. However, that all quickly ended. I insisted my story was true.

Here is that blasphemous essay that placed a psychological question mark on my *permanent record.*

Bloody Boots

Life is not always what it seems.
Often a child will be more open to strange
or unexplainable events simply because
they have never been told
*that can't happen.*

There is another world,
a spiritual world.
A world that only a few will ever know.

Dare to touch that world.

At the age of five, a child's world is filled with fantasy and wonderment. It's a place where anything can happen.

Nothing is impossible. Reality for the little one is formed within the mind. So, what's so strange about a little boy seeing someone whom no one else can see? Many children have imaginary friends – another child, a favorite cartoon character, even an animal. Maybe it's not so strange. Maybe it's just a needed friend for a lonely soul.

It all began very innocently with an early morning discussion about an imaginary friend's late night visit to this five year old's bedroom. "I had someone come to see me last night," he shared over breakfast with his family. The morning paper must have been more interesting. No one seemed to hear.

"He's my friend," the boy continued, "and he said he will be coming back."

And he did come back. As the days went on, the boy's comments at breakfast became progressively more detailed. "He's a big kid, almost a grown-up. He likes my drawings. He wears really thick glasses. He used to sleep in my bedroom. He really liked to hunt, when he had arms. He wears bloody boots."

The newspaper dropped from in front of the boy's parents. His brother responded with a sneer, "He's crazed, make him stop!"

*Bloody Boots*, as he became known to only the family, made regular visits in the middle of the night to the little boy's room. The boy considered Boots his best friend and talked to him about everything. They got to know each other very well, telling stories and laughing throughout the night. At least that was what the boy would tell.

The parents became more concerned as this fantasy grew in detail and importance to the boy. It had even reached the point where the boy was waking everyone in the house at all hours of the night with the sounds of talking and laughter coming from his room.

The boy wasn't growing out of it, as suggested by a family friend.

Finally one night the boy's mother came to his room during a conversation with Boots. But, as she entered the room, Boots quickly excused himself. "They wouldn't understand," he said to the boy.

"See, no one is here. You're going to have to stop making this stuff up!"

It was getting a little old.

"But, Mom," the boy said. "I'm not making it up. See, the pictures I drew for him are gone. He liked them so much he took them with him." The crayon drawings were on his night stand when she tucked him into bed earlier that night, of that she was sure.

"Okay, what did you do with them?" She couldn't find them anywhere.

Breakfast the next morning was different. Instead of ignoring his stories, everyone was listening. The issue of those drawings made everyone's skin crawl.

"Bloody Boots grew up in our house before we moved here," the boy explained. "He went to a war and stepped on a land mine. That's why his boots are bloody."

The boy's father stopped him there, "How do you know what a... What is a land mine, son?"

"It's a bomb the enemy plants underground and ..."

"Okay, okay. I understand," his dad replied.

The boy continued, "Well, he really liked hunting. His rifle is still here, in the den closet."

Of course his father looked, at least half heartedly. He saw nothing. "That boy has some imagination. I just don't know where he gets this crap."

But, what about those drawings?

Weeks passed and the imaginary friend was still a part of the boy's nights. The family decided to just continue to ignore his stories of Boots. Surely he will grow tired of this fantasy. Surely he will grow out of it.

In a small town, everyone knows everyone, and their business. One day while the boy and his mother were downtown shopping, a woman approached and asked, "So, how do you like living at the old Haskin's place? You know, it was the best thing for old lady Haskin to move out of there. She's crazy you know. Mad. Ever since the death of her son."

The blood rushed from the mother's face. "Her son?"

"Yes," the woman continued. "Poor thing, he joined the army to fight in the Korean War. Not over there a week and killed."

"Killed?" the mother cried out.

"Oh, it was terrible, you know. He stepped on a land mine, poor thing. Of course it was closed casket. Oh and what makes it even worse, he should have never been allowed to join. You know, poor thing was legally blind. The boy, he wore these thick glasses... Are you alright? You look as if..."

Without another word the mother turned and ran out the door with her son in tow.

That night the den closet was emptied. Everything. There, on the top shelf, wedged way in the back was a gun. His rifle, just as the boy had said.

"See, he told me it was still here!"

And so was Boots.

Boots continued to visit throughout the years that the boy lived in that house. As the boy grew older, however, the visits left him with a haunting feeling. A feeling that he had been touched by another world.

A spiritual world.

Bloody Boots was just a lonely soul looking for a friend. I know. I was that five year old boy.

Yes, the story is true and still to this day, late at night, a rush of cool air can be felt as the sound of footsteps echo from *my room.*

The story *is* true. But what was I to do when confronted with the option of taking the easy way out? I took the high road and stood my ground. Mrs. Wolfe would never allow such filthy lies in her classroom. Off to the office we went. Just as luck would have it, the district's social worker was in the building. After a drawn out interview, there were serious concerns that *must* be addressed. My parents were called in to meet with my principal, the social worker and Mrs. Wolfe.

What a day from hell in the memoir of my young life. That was the day I was taught *the lesson*. – Avoid the truth if it's going to make someone feel uncomfortable. Dear God, I hope our schools have moved beyond that curriculum by now. But, there was another lesson taught that day. The total, unconditional love and support of my family.

Standing there, in the principal's office, my dad defended my honor, with confidence. "If the boy says it's true, it is true!" What a rare opportunity to hear my dad say something so meaningful. It was on that day manhood took his first step into my soul.

I gazed out the window of the train at a hillside vineyard being worked by what appeared to be a father and his young son. The Italian countryside is such a peaceful place, I appreciated. I recalled the day my dad taught me to ride a bike. That's a picture I will cherish forever. – Unexpectedly, that thorn pierced my senses once again; there was something deeper to be uncovered. Something at the core of my struggles. Without that knowledge, my battle would surely be lost.

When are lessons typically learned, but in times of crisis. My senior year of high school was one of those times. I was constantly split between being a social animal and needing to get away and think. I was the class president, while at the same time being the deep kid who pondered the infinity aspect of God and our universe. But the best times were experienced with my buddy Düp. We had known each other since pee-wee league baseball, and best friends from that first encounter.

We were yin and yang. He was the tall athletic stud and I was the smart kid who had personality. Together, we were complete trouble. I would think up the next crime of the century and Düp would pull it off. My favorite being the time I dared him to streak naked across the high school gym. He did it. And I got it all on 35mm, including the looks of shock and amusement on our classmate's faces. Great shots! We both ended up in the principal's office. Mr. Sheskey knew about our arrangement, as we had been there before. The film was confiscated, but we were let off the hook. He acted tough, but Mr. Sheskey really did have an appreciation for our escapades. Funny is ageless.

But the best times were when Düp and I would load up in my Camaro for a late night cruise on the back roads. I preferred weed and Düp liked his Pabst. Together we were a party on wheels. Those celebrations would often turn to soul searches along the side of some dirt road with a moonlit view. Düp and I would share our deepest secrets, and our worst fears. Sitting there in the deafening silence of the black of night, we would laugh for hours. And sometimes we would cry.

Every spiritual warrior needs a friend like Düp. He taught me how to be free.

There was, however, one secret never permitted to be shared with Düp. – That *horrific realization* mangled my senses. Vertigo rushed me with the force of a deadly tsunami. I frantically shuffled for my Bible. I needed to hear God's voice. *Now!*

Slashing through the pages of the New Testament, I landed on 1 John 2:18.

> Dear children, this is the last hour; and as you have heard that the antichrist is coming, even now many antichrists have come. This is how we know it is the last hour.

My *curse*, profoundly repressed for all these years, arose from the depths of hell.

That dreadfully vivid childhood nightmare.

I am the chosen one…

*I am the antichrist.*

# chapter seven

"You look pale, my son. Are you alright?"

At the very moment my curse oozed its way out of some dark recess in the far reaches of my mind, Silvio made another grand entrance. His timing was horrible. I caught my breath and dried the sweat from my forehead. While pulling down the window to get some fresh air, I explained that I'd be fine in a moment. The memory of some old ghosts had just thrown me for a loop.

"I have just the thing," he thought aloud. "Be right back."

*The antichrist?*

How in the hell had I so completely blocked that trepidation from my conscious mind? Of course I don't *really* believe I'm the antichrist. I'm nowhere near cunning enough to pull that one off. Not that I'd want to! But, why had I buried this lurid thought for so many years? Hidden away in oblivion, never to be heard from again. Well, until now. I was consumed by the ghastly thoughts flying rampantly through my mind. For most of my youth, that irrational fear possessed me. Thoughts of being the *frickin' Spawn of Satan*.

The recollection of this deranged delusion surrounded me in an aura of black. It was like staring head on into a bloody traffic accident. The sounds of screeching tires and breaking glass filled my head. No wonder I had buried it. But what if I were *created* to be the antichrist? My stomach churned as it brimmed with acid.

To even entertain such a concept, one must first believe in the existence of the devil as an actual entity. It had only been a matter of months since I had this very debate with one of my business associates. Joe was a little older than me, and possessed a solid intellectual knowledge of the Bible. Yes, I would cross that line and commit the crime of speaking of God in the workplace.

I would go to him with many a question regarding God. I always enjoyed his views and respected his intellect, though often didn't agree with his findings. Sometimes it was just for the pure enjoyment of a good debate that I would raise controversial religious issues. In this particular case, however, he assured me the devil is not real.

"It's a Biblical metaphor that expresses the evil nature found within every man. Our selfish nature is what fuels the atrocities of this world. Not some villain with a pitchfork."

I disagreed with him and proposed that his thinking was more in line with that of a Freudian view of religion. Handily, I recalled a favorite Freud quote from my college days in Professor Sarver's psychoanalysis course.

But we know that, like gods, demons are creations of the human mind (Freud, 1913).

To support my perspective, I opened Internet Explorer and Googled Bible + Devil. My first hit was the first reference to the devil in the New Testament; Matthew 4:1.

> Then Jesus was led by the Spirit into the wilderness
> to be tempted by the devil.

If we were to look at this statement with Einstein's method of viewing the world, everything is a miracle or everything is not, what would be the *con*verse of this verse?

> Then Jesus (a prophet, not a real god) was led by the
> Spirit (which is actually nothing more than the inner
> voice of one's intellect, or lack of intellect) into the
> wilderness to be tempted (arguably a relative term)
> by the devil (who is really nothing more than an icon
> we created to use as our scapegoat).

Yes, I have a knack for the use of sarcasm for the sole purpose of flustering my opponent. And Joe was an easy one to fluster. Still, my point stands. Once we take the existence of the devil out of the equation, we begin to infringe upon the divinity of God.

Silvio returned with a bottle of Russian vodka and a liter of Orangina, a regional favorite and the perfect vodka shot chaser. That Silvio, he sure knows how to console a guy.

"It's exceptional vodka. I picked it up directly from the distiller in Moscow. I was just there. I had business to attend to at the Kremlin." He laughed wildly at his own stupid little joke. "Did I mention that I serve as a *translator*?"

We both proceeded to our established smoking area and I grabbed the bottle from his hand. That's why he brought it. At this point, I was not prepared to be *all polite*. My worst possible nightmare had just been realized and I needed a drink.

The *antichrist?*

I was in no mood for conversation. Silvio seemed to pick that up rather quickly. He graciously gave me my space. No words were spoken for our entire first cigarette. I wasn't thinking, period. I couldn't even tell you if I took two, three or four pulls off that bottle of vodka. It was good vodka.

I was in a haze so deep that when Silvio finally spoke, it caught me completely off guard; I didn't realize he was anywhere near me.

"So, do you want to talk about those demons you have hidden in your closet? I mean your ghosts."

He had it closer to right the first time, I told him.

"All this talk of the Universe can certainly stir one's soul," he said condescendingly.

I'm so over talking about **God** as the Universe. *The Universe* is so *politicallyfuckingcorrect!* Actually, the thought of it made me nauseous. Plus, the vodka shots mixing with my stomach acid were doing a number on me. The Universe is so damn safe. No one is threatened, no one offended. More lies in those fucking little boxes, all lined up in our perfectly groomed suburban neighborhoods.

I guess it was my turn to go on a rant. Silvio served as the ideal audience. He owed me one.

We speak of God on Sunday, and then leave His sanctuary to put on the *armor of political correctness.* We abandon God at church, where He belongs, entering the world to never fully tell the truth. We follow the ranks of the masses that, too, are programmed by the goals set forth for a consumption-based society. We proudly wear our blinders to the plight of those in need while marching to the beat of ringing cash registers.

We have lost our identity to group-think. Nationalism based on left and right – not right and wrong. Us and them. And everyone wants *you* to be just like *them*. If you don't oblige, then you're separated out, or worse, ridiculed for your *difference*. Individuality has been crushed by our family and friends, our government and church, and our neighborhood and workplace.

We're all too damn terrified to be who we truly are!

"Who's got you all worked up, Daniel?"

God. God had me all worked up! I needed to make a turn, a change of heart. If I only interact with the Universe, how could I ever hope to truly establish a personal relationship with my Creator? The words I choose to speak each day should reflect my knowledge of God, not the Universe. And what about *Jesus*?

Silvio physically cringed as the name *Jesus* rolled off my tongue.

People do that, all the time. Maybe you just did it too. It's that kind of name. The *name above all names*, but we're too damn afraid to use it – at least in positive ways. God help us all.

We don't even have Christmas parties in our homes anymore. They're holiday gatherings. Our efforts at the separation of church and state have removed the name Jesus from our social vocabulary, legally and emotionally. Even your standard, everyday Christian avoids its use at all cost. Well, except on Sundays or possibly at a funeral. You surely don't want to offend anyone.

Why does that name make people feel so ill-at-ease? Is it that it conjures up visions of Jehovah's Witnesses knocking on our doors? Or, does it have to do with its ability to drive a thorn of guilt in our sides? It's just that kind of name. Totally emotionally charged. It makes people react. It makes people think. And, for the most part, we just don't want to think about that kind of stuff.

I swear we get the wrong impression about J.C. But no wonder! The church is more interested in persuading its membership to a particular set of denominational guidelines than to what He actually taught. Jesus was so radical that the Pharisees of His day couldn't contend with His message. Hell, the church today can't even take Him at His Word.

I realized this long and winding walk down memory lane had taken its toll on me. I was fried. Beat down. Weak. I reached toward Silvio to take the bottle from his hand for one final swig. I probably didn't need another shot, but I also didn't really give a rat's ass.

"Take my advice. Put those thoughts out of your mind. You're on holiday, my friend. Take this time to relax. In due time your answer will come. I'm just concerned you may be looking to the wrong source of truth."

Right, Silvio wasn't the one who was just re-informed of his status as the antichrist. There's some perspective for you, buddy. Of course, I wasn't about to share that part of my story with him. That would simply be ludicrous.

My reconnect with God was becoming very real, and real necessary. All things considered, I was prepared to take that turn seriously. But Silvio was right. I needed time to regroup. Lugano was but a few hours away and nothing was going to get in the way of my perfect weekend in paradise. I'll chill for now and pick up the soul search on Monday.

The stress of my recent travels may have been the cause of my concave thinking. Regardless, going forward, my decisions will be made with consideration for my *neighbor*. The *do un* way of living. That's a good first step, I thought to myself.

"You will find your first step soon enough. The first step to finding your source of strength, that is."

I was taken aback. What, now he's reading my mind and answering my thoughts?

"Some of us have been called to serve as translators, while others, as warriors. Yet some will grow to become leaders of the new world order. Change is at hand!"

What the *hell?* Translator, warrior, leader, the new world order! What's the point of your shit, Silvio?

"You can pretend as long as you like, but eventually you must fulfill your destiny, my son. Remember, the challenge is imminent and you are a warrior. The battle is awaiting your cry."

Awaiting me? Please! Get to the point already, I barked. I'm lost. Do you wanna tell me what in the hell you're talking about?

"Your gift. Your calling. Your mission. Why do you think we're here? It's not by chance. It's all part of the plan. And you, my child, are central to the plan."

I'd reached my breaking point. This encounter had become too much to tolerate. I was overcome with fury. Not just at Silvio, but this whole damned experience. I could feel my cheeks turning flush and the sweat begin to bead in the palms of my hands. Who is this guy, acting all worldly and wise, getting in my face about my role in *his* delusion?

My skin crawled with disgust. If I open my mouth now, that all too familiar fury from within my bowels will surely erupt, taking out anyone within screaming distance. And Silvio just stood there, donning that damn smirk. Like he knew exactly what I was feeling inside.

"You must face it, my son. You've known it since childhood. *Didn't you?* Then why can't you just come out? Take your responsibility like a man. This is your destiny, Daniel. And don't worry; you will live a life that is well beyond anything you've ever imagined. You see, my dear protégé, you are one of the lucky ones. You get it all."

I finally let go of my tongue. All I was capable of assembling into a complete sentence under such psychological distress was, "*Who are you?*"

Silvio took a deep breath before revealing his truth.

"I am *Lucifer*, and you are *my son*."

# chapter eight

I awoke, held down by restraints, in Ward Nine of Zurich's
Burghölzli Mental Hospital, the sector for the criminally insane.

Ok, I'm just messing with you. But a psych ward may have been
the safest place for me and Lucifer. I nearly reached the point of
strangling Silvio, that crazy bastard. I wanted to. Seriously. I felt
that much rage. Anger like nothing I'd ever experienced. A
profound, thick disgust. One so repulsive it could be tasted in my
mouth. In that moment of wrath, I hung the culpability for all the
world's evils directly on one explicit entity – *Silvio*.

But, I walked away. I turned from evil and walked away. The
evils in my life were becoming more apparent, too. Maybe the

wrath I placed on Silvio was truly the hatred seething from my own sin. I already knew that this unfortunate introduction to Silvio would haunt me for many years to come. Like that of waking from a nightmare in a cold pool of sweat. To escape that agony, one must get out of bed to disconnect from those demons of sleep. Yet there was no escaping Silvio, as he was destined to be my demon of consciousness.

I settled back into my seat and focused my full attention on the approaching village outside my open window. The summer breeze remains cool at these altitudes, which produced a calming York's Peppermint Pattie effect. In the village center just outside my window, high above the rustic stone shops and cottages, a single church steeple reached toward the heavens. There, resting atop its apex, a rusty iron cross. A single ray of sunlight found a way to reflect off the pitted surface of that old rugged cross, striking me directly in the eyes. I felt a slight sense of hope from that light.

Still, I wanted off this frickin' train. Thankfully, there was only another twenty minutes until we reached Lucerne, my fifth and final transfer – and Silvio's final destination. Amen! In a couple hours time, beautiful Lugano would be mine.

You know, I'm pretty damn good at reading people. There have been instances where I've freaked out perfect strangers by my ability to read their lot in life. My visions go a little beyond intuition, bordering on psychic. I can't explain how I do it and sometimes I'm wrong. But it happens. Perhaps Silvio's *son* thing was simply a fitting statement to conclude our spiritual excursion. He probably just read my fears. I was susceptible; he'd already freaked me out by all the talk of good and evil, then *Lucifer*.

Like the average person, I was immediately drawn into denial. Well, that was my first attempted diversion. It didn't work. It's pretty damn hard to deny my *antichrist* revelation just prior to Silvio's claim that *I am the Son of Lucifer*. Yet, that didn't necessarily mean anything, I kept telling myself.

Rationalization. That was the next defense mechanism put into play to explain it all away. See, I'm really not that bad a person. Certainly no devil. In fact, I'm known to do some pretty selfless acts of kindness. I did a random search of my memory in an effort to find validation. I truly am a humane and caring individual. Not the *Son of Lucifer*, as Silvio had portrayed. The first thing that came to mind was Tim and Benny, better known as *Old School*, back in the Short North.

My home in Columbus is the Short North Arts District, an historic neighborhood located immediately north of downtown and just a few blocks south of the OSU campus. Once known to be the seediest neighborhood in the city, it now hosts some of the most sought after real estate in the Midwest. The Short North has become the city's entertainment heartbeat. Trendy shops, art galleries, hot nightspots, and fine dining options beyond imagination make up the pulse of The ShoNo. Its red brick streets and turn of the previous century architecture gives one a taste of SoHo in Ohio. A very friendly version of SoHo. It's the kind of place that draws diversity and welcomes all.

I own a corner apartment in the Parkview Condominium, overlooking Goodale Park on one side and the downtown skyline of Columbus on the other. With some unit price tags running upwards of three million dollars, Parkview offers a rich mix of nearly famous, famous and infamous characters. The penthouse occupant, the owner of the world's largest used car dealership, told me he was glad to have me living in *his* building. "We need *your kind* of people here," he said in a patronizing tone. I wasn't sure if he thought I was gay, radical, twisted, or what. I'm commonly wrongly accused of many things.

Living at Parkview was exceptional, a dignified and neighborly place to call home. The guy next door and I became fast friends as soon as he moved in. The Reverend Jeb Magruder invited me over for martinis the first night in his new place. Jeb was easily a good 30 years my senior, but that didn't stop us from becoming close buds. He was quite the character, something he would often say about me. We were like twin sons of different generations.

Jeb is best known as President Nixon's number four man in the Whitehouse, and one of the five that did federal time for Nixon's sins following the Watergate break-in. Jeb had some great stories and one of a kind memorabilia from those days. We would sit and talk for hours. He shared the wisdoms of one who had been there. I would listen to his every insight. From his wisdom, it was evident Jeb had unintentionally experienced both sides of life.

Just before leaving on this business trip from hell, Jeb and I had dinner at Hyde Park. Dinner is always at 5:00, even if Hyde Park doesn't offer an early bird menu. Jeb just likes to dine early. Me, I prefer the European dinner hour, sometime after eight. As usual, our evening was delightful – and funny. That Jeb has a devilish sense of humor. That night, Jeb left me with a valuable nugget of knowledge, "I know what it's like to be in the King's Court, as well as in the gutter outside the kingdom walls. The true measure of a man is found in his ability to pick up the pieces after a personal disaster and reclaim his purpose in life."

Jeb is obviously a man of true measure, and wealth. After prison, he attended seminary to become a Presbyterian minister. In more recent years, he became an extremely successful non-profit fund raiser. His way of giving back, he explained. Jeb lives the good life. And he's a good friend. You know, when I get back I need to ask him about life in the Whitehouse during the Viet Nam Era.

But, I had other friends in the Short North. You might call them *the least of these*. I guess Claire continues to have an influence on my life. I became good friends with a couple of homeless guys who lived in Goodale Park, Tim and Old School.

Old School's the wiry and mournful straight man type, while Tim, the jovial orator. Tim was white, Old School black. Proof that homelessness is not prejudice. Thankfully, neither is friendship.

The two of them made quite the team. Our relationship started off slowly, with a dollar here and there. However, our alliance quickly strengthened once I defended their honor with some college kids trying to steal the evening's earnings from Tim's paper cup.

My date for the night thought I had lost it, "Why are you bothering with some filthy homeless dudes?"

Tim asked if he could give me a hug and Old School shook my hand in gratitude. Half the cash was mine for the taking. Tim thought it only fair, as I was the one that recovered the evening's take from those filthy rich thieves. I didn't accept the money, and it was the last date with *that girl*.

Old School was the legs of the operation. Tim, a Viet Nam Vet, had lost both his lower extremities in the war. He looked the part of the all too familiar homeless Vet, complete with scruffy beard, long hair, camouflage jacket (proudly displaying the American flag), and a serious drug problem. He admittedly was not the most hygienically oriented person either. "It's hard enough to stay clean on the streets for the guys who have legs." I'm sure that was true in many ways. But Tim always needed a hug. And I always came through for him. Stench and all. It didn't matter. He was my brother.

Tim depended on Old School, and Old School never let him down. One night Old School confided in me, "I'm so shy that I would starve out here if it weren't for Tim. He takes good care of me, so I will always be his legs." Like I said, they made a good team.

Tim called me God's secret agent, a blessing from above. He was the blessing, the most loving man I have ever met. And he was always appreciative of the littlest things I would do for them.

Old School lost his buddy to a drug overdose last December. It was a sad Christmas. Since then, I make a point of regularly seeking out my buddy in the narrows of the Short North. Just to share the love and toss a few bills his way. He's shy and homeless; everybody just walks right past him.

I had to wonder how Tim would measure up, as a man. I mean, does he matter any less just because he didn't find his way out of the gutter? And are we partially responsible for putting him there in the first place? Please dear Lord, don't let us do that to our new generation of Veterans.

I sure hope Tim and Bloody Boots have met up in heaven. I can imagine them comparing war stories and having a blast, running around those streets paved with gold.

Tim and Old School are a good example of how I'm an alright kind of guy. No devil would care for the homeless. Right? That's more than a rationalization – it's the truth, dammit!

This approach to disarming my fears scarcely made any impact. So, what's the deal with Silvio's secrets? My secrets? Am I a spiritual warrior, but for the losing team? The devil's team? Team Satan! Yet, like everything, this can be viewed from a number of slants. I pondered the numerous possibilities as to the significance of this nightmarish incident along the rails to Eden.

His words seemed wise, but each possessed contempt at its core. Silvio's carefully crafted lies. I returned my gaze to the mountainous countryside and began my attempt to solve the mysteries that lie within Silvio's secret.

*If you don't fully know evil, then you will never fully know God.*

Sure, sounds plausible, but dead wrong. God is love! He's not a combination of good and evil. He is holy, I shouted in my head. To fully know God we must fully love God.

Again, I scrambled for my Bible to seek reassurance. I turned to Mark 12, a familiar passage, one I claimed as the foundation of my view of Christianity. In these verses, Jesus is debating with the religious teachers of His day.

> [28]One of the teachers of the law came and heard them debating. Noticing that Jesus had given them a good answer, he asked him, "Of all the commandments, which is the most important?"
>
> [29]"The most important one," answered Jesus, "is this: 'Hear, O Israel, the Lord our God, the Lord is one.
>
> [30]Love the Lord your God with all your heart and with all your soul and with all your mind and with all your strength.'
>
> [31]The second is this: 'Love your neighbor as yourself.' There is no commandment greater than these."

I had no idea that this single passage would render all Silvio's lies meaningless. But it did. Particularly his perspective, *"you must never forget to love yourself first."* The *love your neighbor as yourself* testimonial in verse 31 seriously slaps the source of Silvio's secrets squarely in the face.

I contemplated, is it really that simple? Love the Lord your God with *all your heart* and with *all your soul* and with *all your mind* and with *all your strength*. And love your neighbor as yourself. Ok, not so simple. Damn, when Jesus said it, it sounded so much easier. The good news is He's got our backs. I just thank God He made it real clear as to what is most important to Him.

*There is no commandment greater than these.*

Still, this comfort doesn't satisfy the larger looming question of this journey. Was I chosen to be in the defenses of the evil one?

EDEN

Was I actually an antichrist and this is the moment of my formal induction into duty? Am I the *Son of Lucifer*?

I prayed.

Then it hit me. Maybe, I'm not completely mad. Could it be that I am important enough to God, to His will, His plan for our world, that the devil was spending all this time and effort, for all these years, trying to convince me otherwise?

Evil lives, man. I just looked it squarely in the eyes and don't like what I saw. The only shred of truth to Silvio's statements is that we must be mindful of evil, and then *run like hell*. Evil is everywhere in our universe. If we deny that absolute truth, we are destined for a great fall.

Sitting there with the late day sun beaming in my window, I knew it was time for a change. I was prepared, armed with a new outlook on my life and our world. I was going to make a difference in this world. I had a mission. One hinted at decades earlier. I was prepared for the commitment and sacrifice this new life would require. But please God, can't we just put this off until Monday? I've been looking forward to this weekend since I left Columbus. I really don't need the guilt trip while I'm totally focused on a pleasure filled weekend in *Paradiso*.

I was sure He'd understand.

For the remainder of my trip to Lugano, I made every effort to cleanse Silvio from my thoughts. When we hit Lucerne, Lucifer and I would go our separate ways – for eternity! Me to platform seven for the 05:20 to Lugano, Silvio off to God knows where to lure yet another victim.

Silvio and I spoke few words as we made our way off the train. He told me that I had been an inspiration to him. That I was the first glimmer of hope he had found in his mounting sea of desperation. Through our encounter, he had gained a rare sense of hope. For that brief moment, it felt as if our roles had been reversed.

Standing on that platform, I pledged my final resistance.

The bag *is* empty.

I turned to leave my nightmare behind as it uttered, "I will be in touch with you first thing Monday morning. I must know all about your weekend."

I should never have given him my business card.

I walked away.

# chapter nine

The sun had yet to set. I'd slept solidly from the moment of
departure to the second we pulled into Lugano Station. Gathering
my bags, I shook off the sleep.

Making my way from the platform to the station exit, I was stalled
by a line of little kids, apparently returning from some outing by
rail. They were all holding hands, so no sheep would be lost. I
stood there waiting for this cute little human barricade to pass.
Finally the last little one scooted on by, freeing my way to Lugano.
Adjusting my backpack, I paused for another look at those happy,
chatty little shits. The last in line, a precious *Cindy Lou Who* angel,
turned to me and smiled. I guess my return grin was so big that
she felt obliged to share with me a tiny wave.

For some reason, kids and companion animals really like me.

Still clearing my head from the booze and locomotion-enhanced sleep, which is customary in my European train travels, I emerged from Lugano Station to a brilliantly sunlit picture postcard moment. I shuffled for my sunglasses. Surrounding me, presented in a full palette of pastels, the breathtaking masterpiece of this glorious delight called Eden.

Needing to catch a ride to the other side of the lake, I scouted out the taxi stand. Approaching that line of late model Mercedes, the steeple of San Lorenzo Cathedral appeared, shooting upward from over the lush hillside of green to grace my arrival. It was the only obstruction between me and *Paradiso,* a seductively beautiful sanctuary of blue waters, bluer skies and terracotta tile rooftops.

Why don't we have Mercedes Benz for taxis in the States? I pondered while walking toward the first car in line. Every place I travel in Europe the taxi of preference is a Mercedes. Well, with the exception of Sweden. Volvo is their logical choice.

I jumped in the backseat of the roomy S-Class and directed my driver to take me to the Holiday Inn. Hmm, I've never before had the notion of a *Holiday Inn* and *Mercedes* in the same thought. My driver pulled from the queue.

He introduced himself. "I am Karim, call on me anytime. I will be your personal driver while you are visiting Lugano."

While driving, Karim scribbled down his phone number on a notepad advertising some brand of coffee and handed it to me. He must have run out of business cards. I thanked him for the offer. As is customary taxi repartee, he asked if this was my first visit to Lugano. Upon my response, he told me it surely would not be my last.

"Lugano is that kind of place. Three days is not nearly enough time in *Paradiso*. Once you taste her sweetness, you will always be drawn back to her," he said while maintaining sporadic eye contact via his rearview mirror. "And you are American, no? I would have guessed British, that is until you spoke."

He went on to tell me that he's originally from Iraq, but moved to Lugano years earlier. Our nationalities offered the occasion for unique perspectives on the war in Iraq to be shared. Perhaps Karim was working me for the tip, but his views were certainly moderate. Particularly when compared to the others I've received recently. We joked, *they* should have the two of us sort out the whole damn mess. We'd end this devastating war today! If only it were so simple, we both sighed.

Karim looked to be in his early thirties, prematurely balding on the top and had the warmth of a fuzzy Arab teddy bear. He possessed a gentle, yet confident air. Although he wore a tormented face, he seemed to be a contented man. I asked why he left Iraq. Could it be a sickening three-letter word – war?

"No. That would have been better. My father was killed by Saddam's régime. He was a university professor believed to be part of the anti-government movement. My mother was also taken from me in that attack. Being their next target, I came here to find a new life. Maybe someday I will return, once your Mr. President's war is over," he shared while pulling to a stop in front of Holiday Inn Lugano.

Coming from India where a taxi costs about $20 a day, Swiss prices were a bit of a shock to the system. Karim unloaded my bags as I fingered through my cash of many colors and countries to locate the Swiss francs. My American Express Card fell from my stash in the shuffle. Karim quickly lean down to retrieve it for me. I paid my debt, plus a healthy tip. I believed Karim to be a man of integrity. Glancing at the card, he handed it back.

"Here you go, Daniel."

I wanted to correct him, but realized it really didn't matter.

"Oh, will you need a ride back to the train on Monday? I will take you, my new American friend," he said while counting his take.

I explained that I would need a ride, but to the airport. My flight leaves a little past noon. We made arrangements for him to be back at 10:45 Monday morning. This was the last stop on my world tour, I told him. Well, not exactly. I am fond of connecting through Amsterdam. My last night in Europe will be spent along the Amstel River in that distinctive metropolis abounding with water, taking in the culture and *kind*.

When in Rome...

"I promise to be here. Now that we are friends, I could not let you down."

Karim pulled away. I took a moment to orient myself to the new surroundings. It's quite a different place, especially compared to those I had just visited. Switzerland is perfect, almost too perfect. It's the kind of place you see homeowners in front of their residences sweeping the street clean, daily. The Swiss are way more than a little OCD, if you know what I mean. I swear the country would self-destruct if someone put Zoloft in their water supply. But it'd be a hell of a lot of fun to watch. I do like their approach to trash and recycling collection, however. Just down the street I could see three stainless steel mailbox-looking receptacles, which accept their deposits to be properly stowed underground. So much different than the garbage piles one sees on the streets of Bangladesh and India. But you can be assured, it costs a hell of a lot more than a penny a day for the disposal of the remnants from last night's dinner.

The sun settling into the western sky had just begun to reach the mountain peaks. The soft glow of the sun and its effect on the world around me painted Paradiso a brilliant shade of gold. It felt good to be here. Three days of no business, no politics, no pressures. I turned and headed for the doorway of this weekend's home base.

Holiday Inn Lugano wasn't so bad after all. I mean, definitely nothing like the Taj Mahal Hotel in New Delhi, but clean and friendly. Kinda like staying at your aunt's house. After the check-in process, I headed up to my room for a quick freshening up.

Why is it that we Americas look upon the *bidet* with such disgust? What an ideal invention. There is absolutely nothing wrong with addressing one's personal concerns with such ease. With a fresh shirt, a splash of Gucci Rush and a touch of product in the hair, I was ready to discover Lugano.

It was 21:30 and darkness had conquered the day in my part of the world. On this trip time had lost its control over me. I could no longer determine the time of day without that heavenly ballet of darkness and light. It was 2:00 am in New Delhi and 3:30 pm in the States. I stuffed my watch in the ManhattanPortage bag I was carrying. No constraints on my life until Monday.

Over the past few years, I've developed a fondness for living in a world of darkness. I'd always been one to watch Letterman before retiring. There's nothing like a good laugh to influence one's dreams. Now, I prefer to end my day with a sunrise and sleep until the noon day sun. Business does have a way of interfering with such a lifestyle. I had perfected my excuses for afternoon only meetings. I am so much more productive in the latter hours of the day. Besides, I own the place.

But, this world traveler was becoming weary. Fatigue had infiltrated every layer of my being and the night was just preparing to breathe. Before venturing out into the streets, I decided to stop in the hotel bar for a cappuccino to rejuvenate my soul.

"You look like a fellow who could use a drink. Or, possibly a man whose had a few."

*Angelo* was printed on his corporate issued ID badge, but his voice didn't correspond with the name. He had nothing of an Italian accent to go with that moniker. I asked for an extra strong cappuccino and said he was right about the *few too many*.

"So, this is your first time to Lugano?"

His accent was definitely Eastern European, but his knowledge of the English language, superior. I'd guess he was from somewhere in the more southern regions, like Romania or Bulgaria, given his darker hair and skin tone. Angelo looked to be approaching 40 and displayed a congenial demeanor from behind the bar. But is everyone I meet in this town going to ask if this is my first time?

I explained that, yes, it was my first time; however I would be leaving on Monday. I knew that three days in paradise would not be nearly enough time to enjoy all her charms. I was sure to be drawn back by her splendor.

"It sounds like you have been here before," he said with a smile. "So what brings you to this treasure we attempt to hide from the outside world?"

I told an extremely brief synopsis of my travels and how much I was looking forward to the pleasures of Eden.

"Are you sure you haven't been here before? You even know our nickname for this terrestrial delight."

Ok, I was impressed with the English vocabulary exhibition, but terrestrial delight? Angelo was some character. I explained that I only knew of Eden because of a conversation I had earlier in the day. I gave him the obligatory compliment on his English skills and asked where he'd learned to speak so well.

"I lived in the United States of America in 2000. My home was New Orleans. I bartended in that charming city for nearly a year. Sadly, visa issues forced me to leave. But, I have been in love with American movies, music and literature all my life. I simply love the American way, however that president of yours sure makes you Americans look bad."

I explained the fifteen minute rule. Everyone I'd met on this trip brought up Bush within 15 minutes of meeting me, the damn American. I also told him about Silvio's attack on America that I'd barely survived. So Angelo, I'm avoiding that conversation at all costs.

"I understand. When you're an American, you carry the weight of the world on your shoulders, whether you like it or not. But maybe you should stop trying to be the *world police*."

He almost lured me in. The world police issue has always gotten my dander up. I've never been able to figure out where we got that assignment. The global defender of *freedom* and *democracy* – by whatever means necessary. Maybe it has something to do with the survival of the richest?

"So tell me about this new friend of yours," he said in an attempt to oblige my request for a less controversial conversation.

Yet, another topic to avoid this weekend. I reached for a smoke and shook my Bic to encourage the remaining gases to serve their purpose. This bought me the time to come up with my own diversion. Pretending to have missed his last query, I asked Angelo how he got the name.

"It's not my given name, but I like to adopt a local name to feel more a part of my new culture. When I lived in America, my name was Andrew. Names are a funny thing. They carry with them so much meaning. And you? Your name is Daniel, but you introduced yourself as something else. Why?"

That recently acquired horror erupted, churning in my stomach. I can't take any more of this! I shouted, "What on God's earth do you mean, man?"

"Oh, I am so sorry. I don't mean to pry. We respect one's privacy in Switzerland. I apologize. On your check-in slip brought over from the front desk you are recorded as Daniel. We must remain watchful. There are those who will try to deceive, who will use a fictitious name or room number to steal a drink."

Relieved, I explained my middle name scenario and apologized for the abrupt response. It was just that this guy on the train today had me a little freaked out. Just too many twists of fate for my liking. Part of it had to do with him knowing my first name.

"Isn't it odd how providence finds its way into our lives? Do you believe in coincidences?"

How could I not? Not to get into details, I said, but I do believe in those magic moments in time where events happen that just can't be explained. Given I didn't want to encourage that discussion I moved the conversation along once again. I asked Angelo how he came to live in Lugano.

"It's difficult to provide for one's family in my homeland. But more than that, I was seeking a new life. I am a wanderer at heart. That's why I always work in hotels. I love to be around those who share my passion for life."

Sitting there across the bar from Angelo, I again realized that I too was seeking a new life. I told him I could relate. I was faced with a bit of a life dilemma that had attached itself to me earlier in the day. I was only a little confused. Nothing a weekend in Paradise couldn't cure.

By now, I'd been in town for close to two hours and still hadn't hit the pavement. With the sun already asleep, my stomach was also telling me it was time to move on. Finishing my smoke, I asked him why he chose 'A' names – Andrew, Angelo.

"That's a good question. I just like to start at the beginning. Maybe that's what you should do with your conundrum, brother. Can I get you another cappuccino?"

I'm not sure what made me want to stay. Possibly it was having a sane person to converse with, particularly after spending my afternoon with the *Riddler*. Sure, you know the one. He's that guy who would forewarn Batman of his caper, sending complex clues and word puzzles. I took Angelo up on his offer for a second cappuccino and asked for a shot of whiskey, on the side.

"So I was right on both accounts. You *are* a man who could use a drink. So, where does your story begin?"

He was doing his job and doing it well. The job responsibilities of a bartender are the same wherever you go in the world; to serve and protect the secrets of their drunken clients. However, I'm really not *that* guy. You know the one who goes around telling everyone his life story. I hate that guy. I tend to keep things to myself. I have never wanted to bore others with the details of my life. I prefer to keep my secrets secret. Besides, I knew that my experiences and internal complexities tended to frighten the casual observer.

Angelo leaned heavy on the bar across from me, as I began to tell my saga. It seems my most recent crisis started on September 11, 2001, as it was for many of us. Although only temporary, we became a more loving, caring nation. Patriotism ran warm through the veins of each one of us. Remember the scores of weddings that took place in New York City after 9/11? We were all forced to see evil, day and night, on our television screens and computer monitors. We needed hope. We needed love. Marriage was the answer for some. For me, marriage was not a solution. The hope and love I sought must be found within.

Then it hit me. I was just in London, I told Andrew, Angelo, A' whatever. That was it! My London experience was what brought all this back to light. I was in London a few weeks ago, on July the 7$^{th}$. 7/7 – the U.K.'s 9/11. With so much happening in my life over the past several weeks that day had sadly become old news in my fish and chips paper. I know that wasn't the case for those who had personally experienced the loss of love and peace.

I arrived Heathrow amidst the early morning rush in plenty of time for my late afternoon meeting. Until then, London was mine to discover. In all my European travels, I had yet to step foot in England. Obviously, I'd picked one hell of a day to establish a first impression of British culture.

As the bombs ripped through London's Underground, and life was stolen by religious extremists, I too was using the Tube. Far from the explosions, thank God. In all the chaos, I found myself in Bloomsbury. As fate would have it, while walking toward Tavistock Square thinking the terror had ended, the final blast of that horrific day slashed open a double-decker bus right before my eyes. At final count, that attack murdered fifty-two people and injured 700. To what end?

Reflecting on what I had observed, there was only one logical conclusion to draw. Evil is everywhere. I've lived it on this journey – from poverty to political uprising to terrorist attacks. I somehow felt a personal responsibility for those sins against humanity, yet wasn't quite sure why. Maybe it was that evil lived in me, too.

The hurt of that day could be seen on Angelo's face. "Horrifying. Sadly another example of the pain our world is facing," he shared.

9/11 left me seriously wounded. I didn't sleep or eat well for months after that day. I carried the hurt of those who experienced a personal loss from that unthinkable tragedy. And I cried for our world. Evil had reached a new level of wickedness, one that was sure to breed – a pandemic of hatred. I told Angelo I felt deep in my heart that we are living in the days of a new holy war.

While still coping with our world's agony, I was clobbered with one much closer to home. The passing of my stepfather. I really didn't anticipate my reaction to this personal loss. However, the unexpected death of the *Chief* left me to re-evaluate life's priorities. Those of love, concern, meaning, and purpose. Looking back, the most difficult part of my loss was experiencing the pain of my mom, who had her best friend die in her arms.

Still, there were positive events that led me to this life dilemma. Interestingly, one of those events was *Bonnaroo*. Angelo looked perplexed, like he should know the meaning of this English word.

Bonnaroo, which actually means nothing, is a music and arts festival that takes place each summer in the rolling hills near Manchester, Tennessee. Just an hour south of Nashville, this 80,000 person, 10 stage, four day festival is held on a farm Woodstock style. Amazing artists like Ben Harper, Jack Johnson, James Brown, Neil Young, Lucinda Williams, and The Dead entertain from noon to 4:00 a.m. each day. It was there that my life as a successful businessman first came into question.

I had spent my entire life building my personal kingdom of wealth and possessions. I started at an early age, selling seeds and greeting cards door-to-door when only seven. From there, fully enamored with the goodies that cash could buy, I set out to acquire, consume and live my life my way. Money alone wasn't enough. I wanted to grow intellectually as well. Knowledge is power.

Throughout recent years I kept seeking and searching. Still no real joy seemed to be available to me. However, at Bonnaroo I felt a real sense of happiness from within. There, no one was discussing stocks and business strategies, or bragging about their fine *anything*. It didn't matter what you *do* or how much money you *make.* An attitude of peace, love and music abound. I was free at Bonnaroo, free to be the real man that I truly am.

It was there, at Bonnaroo, while pondering the loss of the Chief, that which truly matters in life was revealed to me. It was time for a change, time to seek true love and true freedom. To live in a way that reflects my *real self,* not the self formed by the expectations of this world. However, upon returning to my *real life* in Columbus, I replaced the insights found in those hills of Tennessee with uncertainty. An unfamiliar emotion for me.

So Angelo, here I am years later, still seeking and still fighting. Even with all that I have and all that I am, I know there is some sort of hole inside of me. And that hole has allowed my happiness to escape. Maybe it's the evil that lives in me, but I just don't *feel* anymore. I'm not looking for sympathy, bro. I'm confident the answers will come in their own time.

"I see many a man walk through that door. Each with his own set of angels and demons. The ones that are most capable of dealing with their spirits are the ones who have found their purpose. And that purpose never has anything to do with personal wealth, my brother. Keep that in mind as you walk this earth."

Ok, no more downers Angelo. I'm here to have fun!

"Well, maybe you just needed to free a little angst before embarking on your holiday. What are your plans for the evening?"

*Ristorante al Portone* had been recommended to me, I told Angelo while gathering my things. It was suggested that I arrive around 23:30. The guy who introduced me to this establishment knows the proprietor, a gentleman by the name of Damiano. Perhaps you know him.

"*Damiano* – not a friend of mine."

I charged the drinks to *Daniel's* room and gave my brother Angelo a good tip. I asked him for general directions to *al Portone*. As long as I get sent off in the right direction, I'm usually pretty good at finding my way.

I wished him farewell and headed for the door. What a gentle soul that Angelo. He said something in Italian as I opened the door to Eden. I didn't even try to catch it, but his grin made it seem like I should've given it at least a little effort.

Speaking for me this time, Angelo said, "I will say to you that which my father tells me as I go out." With a sincere gaze, he offered, "May God's love be with you."

The hour had gotten late. It was nearly 11:00 and my stomach was wrenching from hunger. I considered pulling Karim's card from my bag, but knew the thirty minute stroll to the other side was more what I needed.

The moonlit walk along Lugano's tree lined promenade was enchanting. The disseminating moon reflected off the waters and lit my way along the lakeshore. It was everything I had imagined, and more. The Travel Channel did a great job of capturing the essence of this place, but to truly know Eden one must jump in with both feet. The immense beauty and brisk night air tripped my senses and awoke my being. I was no longer weary. I was invigorated, alive.

The temptation to route myself through the *Piazza della Riforma* was overwhelming, but I resisted. I will savor that morsel as my dessert after this highly anticipated epicurean orgasm. I love the central gathering places sporadically positioned throughout European cities. And *Piazza della Riforma* offers a unique glimpse into Lugano's culture and cuisine. At least that's what Samantha Brown said in her travelogue.

I arrived at *Viale Cassarate*, 3. Between Angelo's assistance and my superb sense of direction I didn't miss a step. *Ristorante al Portone* looked to be on the expensive side of the isle, but this was my holiday. I was ready to indulge, long into the night. I opened the door to the familiar sound of a tinkering bell, one more likely to be heard at a butcher shop. Not what one would expect at an exclusive bastion of *Nouvelle Italiana*. Still, it was nice.

"*Buona sera,*" a truly Italian gentleman shouted as I entered the establishment.

*Buona sera signore*, I replied with my best Italian accent.

He began speaking in English.

"Welcome to *Ristorante al Portone* and good evening. How may I be of assistance to you, sir?"

I explained that *al Portone* came highly recommended and that I was to be sure to introduce myself to *Damiano*.

"Daniel, my friend, come in. We have been waiting for you. I am Damiano. And no, you my friend, you come highly recommended. Silvio told us all about you. I am honored to serve you this evening."

Restaurants are my weakness. I love them, sitting at the bar of the most exquisite dining locale in a city and meeting the rich and famous. Mostly for good company and interesting stories, but in part because they think the same of me. Apparently Damiano did hold me in high regard, as the premier eight top in the back of his place was prepared just for one. A bottle of Ketel One on ice also awaited my arrival. I didn't realize I'd even mentioned my preferred vodka to Silvio, that thoughtful fool.

Damiano directed me to take my place of honor.

"Eat, drink and be merry, for it will benefit us all. Tonight's affair is compliments of Silvio, our dear, mutual associate."

# chapter ten

Sitting on my throne, the regal wait staff of *Ristorante al Portone* tended to my every need. I was not offered a menu, as the evening's fare would be personally selected by the chef. His choice, a sampling of nearly every item on the menu, intermixed with a few delectable treats that were not. With each course came a flight of regional and international wines to complement his creations. *Ristorante al Portone* was turning out to be more than I could have ever imagined. All compliments of Silvio, that eccentric jester.

I am the *King of Lugano*; I celebrated stuffing myself beyond capacity. What a culinary climax, the absolute best I'd ever experienced. So fun. I wished my friends from home could see me now. Better yet, I'd love to share this moment with them. I was demanding the attention of not only the restaurant service team, chef and owner, but the other patrons as well. All the fuss over Damiano's special guest had the restaurant abuzz.

They obviously had no idea, it was *only* me.

Often times, people think I am someone that I am not. Like a celebrity or something. I have that look. The look like you should know who I am. Or perhaps, we may have known one another in a past life or something. I get the "you know who you look like" from strangers quite frequently. My top three, Elton John (*how gay*), Stephen King (*pretty scary*) and Michael Myers as the *International Man of Mystery*, Austin Powers. I like that one.

*Yeah baby, yeah.*

Thankfully, I only had time to consume a single Ketel One, tonic and lemon before the rush of food and wine began. By the end of my courses, I couldn't have forced another bite. However, an after dinner drink would be delightful. Taziana, a sexy little Italian *bella* and my pick of the night from Damiano's staff, said she knew just what I desired. If only she really did.

To my displeasure, Damiano returned with a bottle and port glasses in hand. Four of them. Taziana gave me the sad face look from across the room. Her boss had the honors.

"Daniel, tonight I have an exclusive treat for you," he said while presenting a bottle of *Ferreira Duque De Braganca Colheita Port,* circa 1900. "This extremely rare tawny is dry and soft, with a very sweet bouquet. However, its lovely aftertaste is this vintage's most captivating feature. If it would be your pleasure I shall also like to offer you some company."

My fingers were crossed; possibly Taziana was the company he spoke of. Due to the matter of those four glasses, I was assuming my odds were slim.

"I would like to introduce two highly regarded and very affluent members of our community. I have known these gentlemen for a number of years and am confident you will find them to be agreeable conversationalists. They both lead interesting lives."

Damiano motioned to the gents who had been sitting at the bar since the time I was on my second or third course. I am extremely aware of my environment.

"Gentlemen, I have the honor of introducing you to Daniel. As you know, a man who has already gained the respect of some very influential people. Daniel, this is Sa'eed and Colsante."

We all shook hands while exchanging greetings and then settled in for our after dinner sips, a few smokes and what was sure to be some interesting international tête-à-tête. This really was some night.

Our conversation was stimulating; the 100 year old port, something only a privileged few would ever have the pleasure to enjoy. And I found the company of Sa'eed and Colsante to extend the kind of connection I require to offer friendship.

Sa'eed, the Managing Director for Funds Management with Banque UniSuisse, had lived throughout the world and was a collector of ancient artifacts. Colsante was a much quieter fellow who didn't offer to tell how he spent his day. He did share that his lineage dated back to the early elite of the region now known as Switzerland, which may explain why how he spends his day is of little consequence.

Damiano excused himself, as he had a restaurant to run. I offered my friends to join me in a Ketel One; I was switching it up. I've experienced a port-induced hangover only once before, but never again. One glass is my max.

Colsante was still finishing his glass while Sa'eed accepted my vodka offer and said, "So Dan, tell us a little about yourself. Are you married, kids?"

I quickly alerted my new friend that it was Daniel, not Dan. Given there was no crucial reason not to play along I decided tonight I would be Daniel. I am totally not a Dan.

I explained I was married once, back in the early 90s. It didn't take. Actually, that was the longest 18 months of my life. El had her demons, and my spirits just couldn't seem to play nice with hers. Neither did those of her first husband. Good guy, he served a longer sentence than me. Funny, she and I were old grad school buddies and even remained friends after our divorce. Well, until recently. I had become the focus of El's wrath over the past year or so. For what reason, I may never know. She certainly can cop an attitude. It was then I began calling her *El Diablo*, just for fun. I know she'll come around. El truly does have a wonderful heart, even if it is hard to see at times. Regardless, I have been continually blessed by that error in judgment. Their names are Shea, Noah and Drew, my ex-stepkids.

I found myself speaking like a proud father, even if it really isn't the case. They are incredible kids, smart, charming and socio-politically active. A quality they got from their mom. When I came around, they were all still babies. Shea was five, Noah, three, and Drew, still in diapers.

I couldn't help but pull out my wallet to show pictures of my kids.

"This is Shea. She'll be a famous author someday. I've known that girl to consume books ever since I met her. She began writing lengthy stories while in the first grade, and she has never stopped writing. Shea completed her high school diploma at Interlochen Arts Academy, a boarding school located on Lake Michigan. Demi and Bruce's kids also went there at the time. Now in university at Kenyon, she will be studying in London next year as an exchange student. I'm so proud of that girl. She was only six years old the day I was assured she would make it in this world. Shea appeared to be a timid child from the outside, but when she asked me to ride the biggest, fastest, up-side-downest coaster at Hershey Park, I knew that kid had the guts to take on the best of them."

I poured a little more vodka as I moved on to Noah's photo.

"Now this is Noah; the only boy and the middle child. What a double curse. This kid handles any situation that comes at him with style and grace. He's a musician and an intellect, and a wry comedian. His best quality in my eyes, he stands for those who have been wronged and isn't bothered by the ridicule that may follow. An all-around incredible kid. He and I have maintained a strong bond throughout the past 13 years. Our styles just mesh. He possesses the calming air of his Catholic father and the radical outlook of his Jewish mother. I hope I contributed to his vast ability to express love. He does have my taste in girls."

Then I pulled the last photo from my wallet.

"And then there is Drew. This beauty was *my* little princess. She possesses talent beyond belief. Drew, too, is a musician and always has been. That girl would sing the scales, in perfect pitch, before she could speak a word. At the age of five she began playing the harmonica. It was then she wrote her first song, lyrics included – *Drew's Blues*. Now barely fifteen, she's an accomplished pianist, has written tons of songs, has an impressive performance schedule, and just released her second CD. Drew has a definite style all her own. Like the song of an angel. A melancholy angel. And nobody better try to change it. That old soul has always had a bit of an independent streak."

Colsante, who was now ready for a Ketel One, responded, "They do sound to be extraordinary children. You gleam as you speak of them. The fact that you've stayed in their lives for all these years is quite a testimony to your character. Those are some lucky kids to have you in their lives."

They are lucky kids, I explained. But it's not because of me; both their parents have always been involved in their lives. I'm the one who's blessed. If it weren't for them, I would never have known the love and joy that only comes from caring for your child. I just hope they think of me as a bonus, and a place they can come if they need me. Like my ole stepdaddy used to say, "It don't gotta be blood to be love."

I returned the favor and asked about their families. Pictures came out and the stories continued into the night.

Sa'eed showed the hospital photo of a newborn baby boy, already with a head full of thick, dark hair. Quite the little man, I told him.

"He's just a week old," Sa'eed explained. "This is my first night out of the house since Celia went into labor. My in-laws have been visiting for nearly two weeks now. They're about ready to push me off the side of the damn mountain. Her mother is making my life a living hell. They are Catholics, from Rome. As you can imagine, my wife has faced serious condemnation from her family for marrying a Muslim."

Sa'eed proudly bragged on of what the future holds for his first born. His was a special boy. One who will someday have the whole world dancing in the palm of his hand, Sa'eed boldly asserted. He then seemed to drift off into a fantasy world. The smile on his face assured it was a happy place.

Colsante took the opportunity to jump in, explaining he was deeply rooted in Swiss culture, but preferred to live in this Italian-influenced region of the country. "I've found the detached open-mindedness of the Swiss society best fits my lifestyle." His wife was originally from Mozambique, a dark-skinned beauty who also preferred Lugano, if she must live in Switzerland at all. "Sonia had difficulty adjusting to the Swiss way of life." He then presented a photograph of his one true joy, Luciana. "She will be attending university in Paris next term," he said with obvious pride. "The Sorbonne."

"Luciana speaks seven languages with impressive fluency," Colsante explained. He'd taught her six of them. "Arabic was her idea, and Sa'eed has been an immense help with that one. We just have a knack for speaking in tongues, one might say."

Our short time together had already created a bond among the three of us. We were all so different, yet shared an unspoken understanding of one another's lives. As the night progressed, we discussed our professions, our views, and our cares. The conversation was intellectual and stimulating, and at times, hilarious. Best of all, the fifteen minute rule was finally broken. No Bu'shit.

Sa'eed pulled a tiny vial from his leather jacket and displayed it underneath the table. "Trust me, it's pure," he said with confidence.

I assumed it was coke, which was all I needed to know. I've seen too many people go down on that shit. That and crystal meth. Like Düp would always say, "That shit's no good for anybody, buddy." I think Sa'eed got the idea from the expression on my face. To be sure, I told him that I prefer to keep it natural. "If you gotta joint, I'd be happy to join."

"Sorry, that's not a product line we represent," Colsante laughingly alleged.

I needed some fresh air anyway. They headed back to the kitchen to do their dirty deed. I walked out to browse the storefronts along *Viale Cassarate*.

Talking about our families added a comforting depth to the evening's conversation. It was enjoyable to hear about the lives of my new international friends. I was really beginning to feel a connection with Sa'eed and Colsante.

I looked to my watch to check the time. It wasn't there. I'd left my mobile at the table, so the hour was still a mystery. I wished I'd brought it out. Talking about the kids made me want to call one of them. On a recent trip to Ibiza, while out partying at a beach club, I drunk dialed Drew just to share the happenings, and the love. She's always teasing me about that call, "You were partyin' like a rock star." What a funny call. It was midnight on the Mediterranean, which was 6:00 in the evening Drew's time. As you could imagine, we were obviously at different points in our day. It's cool, she always reminds me to include her in on my international nights out. What a blessing, that angel of mine.

I wasn't always the best role model for Shea, Noah and Drew, but I was always there for them. Hopefully each of us gained something from the total honesty and unconditional love we share. That makes up for a lot. As it is promised, *Love covers a multitude of sins.*

The restaurant crowd began pouring out of *al Portone*, as it must have been closing time. I headed back inside to meet up with my friends.

"Daniel. We thought you had left us," Colsante said while moving aside so I could regain my place of authority. "And just when the evening was about to get interesting," he bantered.

Damiano dimmed the lights and the room took on a smoldering glow that radiated from the candles stranded on each table, fighting for their final breath of light. Sa'eed told me they'd talked about me while I was outside. "We decided you have something of an aura of truth about you. An element that prods others to expose themselves. That will be very beneficial."

Colsante excitedly jumped in, "Are you familiar with *secret societies?*"

His abrupt subject change was awkward. *Forced.* Of course I was familiar; the Freemasons, for example, a worldwide organization that originated in Scotland during the sixteenth century. Now a global mainstream society, the Masons are known for their secret rituals based on some belief in a generic Supreme Being. However, more recently, Dan Brown's book, *Da Vinci Code,* popularized the mystique of such assemblages. I'm sure they're a fun social network for those who have a need to belong to a group. That's just never been my thing, I insisted. I don't need to belong.

"Belonging for the right reason may change your mind," Sa'eed suggested.

Colsante continued, "Exactly. The Freemasons are a distant cousin of ours, you might say. Over the years, changes became necessary. For a society to maintain its posture, it must continue to expand. This is where you come in. I guess you could say I have a proposition. There is someone I would like you to meet. However, before I get into those details, let me educate you."

I know I said no business until Monday, but I certainly would never miss out on hearing a proposition based on some secret society.

"I'm an ancestral member of a sect within the Swiss Guard called *The Corps of the Pontifical Swiss Guard.* Since their formation in the early 1500s, members of my family have served among the leadership of the Vatican's protectorate. The Pope's personal army," Colsante said with irreverent pride.

Sa'eed smiled, "I know Colsante's family and that's like putting the wolf in charge of the sheep."

We all laughed.

"Similar," Colsante agreed with a half smile. "However from within our sect, a *societates clandestinae* was established. Its origin dates back to the days of Pope Julius II, who was known as the Defender of the Church's Freedom. His devotion was not beneficial to the political structure of the day. Thus, what translates as *The Brotherhood of the Passage* was established within our ranks to protect the rights of the *select*. Still to this day, we stand guard on both the Church and the world. And lucky for you, one must no longer be Swiss to belong."

"They even accepted a damn Saudi into their fold," Sa'eed interjected. "I serve my purpose. An ambassador among our opposing cultures."

I was drawn in, taken by images of those that had come before me, asked to enter the *Passage*. This isn't some fairy tale, this shit's for real!

Colsante leaned forward as if to protect his secret from inquiring minds. "Over the centuries, our brotherhood has become somewhat of a major player in the global community. We offer the most advanced global networks that ensure the seamless transfer of funds and raw materials, in a manner that is discreet. We are trusted among the most powerful men on this planet. Men from every nation. And you could be a player in our web of influence. Perhaps, a key accomplice."

Damiano was back in his office, so the front of the house was completely ours. Sa'eed pulled out the vial of white powder again. This time there was no need for them to escape to the kitchen. Again he offered. I was tempted; maybe just this once, I thought to myself. I could use a little pick me up. It's been a long frickin' day. He tapped out his goods on a plate and crushed the crystals with a credit card. His finished product, a triangle made of shimmering white lines.

While rolling a 1000 franc note, Sa'eed toasted, "May this serve to unite us, a trinity of the brotherhood."

After hearing his pledge, I wanted to back out. But I didn't. I couldn't. He made a toast – *to us*. I wasn't about to insult my new friends and future business partners. So I joined in. It felt great. It was pure. But I didn't like myself much at the moment. I swore that shit off when I was still a kid. Yet, the buzz gave me a rush. It wasn't a jaw-clenching high. It was mentally stimulating, yet physically relaxing.

I asked Colsante if the business of the brotherhood is legal. I had already crossed one line tonight; I certainly don't want to keep heading down that path.

"It's like the internet porn business, not necessarily tasteful, but not necessarily illegal."

I didn't like his example. I've always had issues with gentlemen's clubs and online porn. Don't get me wrong, I believe the woman's body is one of God's most awesome creations. It's what's behind the scenes of porn that bothers me. The personal stories. Where do you think these girls come from? Girls that show their goods for cash. I mean, how many times have you heard a little girl say, "When I grow up, I want to become a *stripper*." Sure, sin pays well. But at what price? That industry supports the continued assault on girls that have most likely already been damaged by a father, or neighbor, or family *friend*. I hurt for those girls. I don't find their tragedy the least bit sexually stimulating.

"My point being, each of us draws a line somewhere between right and wrong. I am only asking you to straddle that line, just a little, for the benefits it will afford us all."

I was feeling at war with myself. With the battle lines drawn, I was on the edge. Or, maybe it was the coke.

"Are you game, my brother?" Colsante reached out for a gentlemen's handshake to make it official. "I can fill you in on the details tomorrow evening at *The Mansion*. There you will meet my uncle. Your selection will require his final approval." He paused, and then repeated his question.

"Are you in?"

I shook his hand.

# chapter eleven

The cool night air and the walk *lungo lago* awaiting me was the ideal way to close out the night. A brisk stroll to Paradiso. What a night it had been, I reflected, replaying the evening's events repeatedly in my head. Damiano insisted I take the remains of the *Ferreira Duque De Braganca Colheita Port,* circa 1900, now safely tucked away in my bag. Sweet deal! And I know just the person who will truly appreciate a glass when I get home. Jeb. He'll know the value of such an offering.

I'd made my way to the promenade before realizing I hadn't walked through *Piazza della Riforma*, my intended route home. That Samantha Brown, she made it seem so damn romantic on the widescreen. I'd love to travel with her. She's kinda hot in a weird kinda way. The buzz had programmed my thoughts to *random*. I could see it, me, Sam and Anthony Bourdain, all hanging out in Nice. I love the South of France. I know this American dude there who opened the first Mexican restaurant in Paris, back in '78. Actually, it was Tex-Mex. He has a place on the *Côte d'Azur* these days, *Texas City Mexican Cantina*. The coldest €10 *Tecate* in all of France. That'd be the trip. We'd make one hellacious trio in Nice.

The early morning breeze whisking across Lake Lugano stirred my senses. I was *alive*. I felt like singing. So I did, in my best Luciano Pavarotti tenor. *I'ma feelin' good and I'ma feelin' fine. I'ma feelin' liberated, I think I'm in-e-bri-ate-did.* Sometimes that's simply a fun word to say. *Inebriated*, I chuckled. My cheek muscles ached from the continual smile that had plastered itself across my face. Ok, so I can amuse myself when left alone. I absorbed my surroundings and tempted the darkness so alive in me.

Night is my favorite season of the day.

This evening had been *way* over the top. Come to think of it, the whole damned day had been total overkill. In the last 24 hours I had met *one* who was escaping, *one* who was wandering, *one* who was experiencing, *one* who was persuading, a *few* who were cute, and the *one*, *diavolo,* شَيْطان, 악마, diabo, şeytan, дьявол, ďábel, διάβολος, or djevel. Whatever the tongue, it's all the same. *Satan.* I met *him* today, too.

*The Mansion.* It even sounds ethereal! But that's where I'm heading tomorrow night. No, tonight! Colsante made it very clear I was going to have the time of my life, in addition to a life changing re-direct of professions. Most importantly, I was going to meet Uncle Nuncio. They would pick me up at The Inn a little before 20:00. Uncle Nuncio doesn't like to wait. Cocktails will be served at 20:30 and dinner sharply at 21:00, just as Nuncio likes it. We would discuss business only upon retiring to Nuncio's personal chambers. I was warned not to speak of Colsante's offer while we were dining. Nuncio never mixes business with his pleasures.

The walk was doing my head good. I was still mentally hyped from the coke and Colsante's incredible proposition. Still, I was looking forward to my bed. I needed to chill. If only I had some pot. That would be the perfect communion with God tonight. I needed that connection with Him. It might sound all Rasta, but when I'm smokin' the bud, I feel a closer union with my Creator. My mind is always a rush of data, words, pictures, and sounds, blocking out that which is of greatest consequence – my visions. I must diminish diversion to fully focus.

The night sky in front of me was still a wash of black. Behind me, just over the peaks, the radiance of morning light prepared to make her scheduled appearance. I love to walk the earth when everyone else is sleeping. It makes me feel like the night belongs to only me. I could hear the music of India playing in my head. I also cherish the night because no one is watching. I danced along the lakeshore, underneath the umbrella of horse chestnut and linden trees, to that rhythmic beat that filled my world. As the sky continued to awaken around me, I awoke to the reality that I was on the verge of something momentous.

A new life.

The day's chilling experiences with Silvio began to find their way back to my conscious mind. I swore to myself I wouldn't think about it until Monday. Although, being introduced as *a man who's gained the respect of some very influential people* indicated my level of involvement in this synchronicitous day.

My curiosity has always gotten the best of me. New experiences are my life's blood. It's like an addiction. And the paradoxical circumstances of this day got me high. I must withhold any judgments, I reminded myself. I'm a rational man. The business prospects of this summit were more than opportune. I really needed a change in direction. An escape from my current life, which continued to eat away at my soul.

The dark side of this parallelism, Silvio, remained a point of contention within my spirit. He certainly did claim to be Lucifer, but was that just a part of his game? A jokester who pegged me as a dupe, for his personal amusement. Obviously, he liked me. He provided an evening in paradise that I would not soon forget.

Morning's arrival in Lugano is always slightly delayed. A reminder of the Italian side of this Swiss town. The reach of the mountain peaks hold off the appearance of the sun a few minutes longer. Lugano's exclusive snooze button. With the onset of morning light, I could distinguish the Grand Hotel Eden off in the distance. Paradiso, I celebrated. Almost home.

As I neared the gardens of Paradiso, the music of guitar and song, in English, tugged at my consciousness. Up ahead was a small group sitting on the grasses alongside a beautifully pruned garden of tulips, rhododendrons, primroses, and begonias. The Swiss love their gardens, particularly in Eden.

They were American. That's refreshing. I hadn't talked with any Americans since I ran into Claudia back in Delhi. It really hadn't been that long ago, it just seemed that way. This colorful group looked the part of the 60s hippie set, protest song and all. Nothin' like a taste of Bob Dylan to warm the soul.

The guitar player was a guy with dreads and a Dylanesque singing voice. He finished the final verse of *The Times They Are A-Changin'* just as I was about to reach their love-in. My *good morning* was returned with, "Hey, you're American!"

I was immediately asked to join their party. I introduced myself and they went around the circle giving me their names. Chels, Phil, Lauren G, and Chachie Longbow, the guitar player. – Names that fit them well. I asked about their travels. Chels quickly informed me they *live* in Paradiso.

My bad for assuming.

"We attend Franklin College Switzerland, a private liberal arts university with an English-based curriculum."

Phil joked that it's a haven for radical rich kids. Lauren G suggested, rich kids with a passion for our world. They did appear to possess a genuine concern for what was happening on our planet, and they possessed the knowledge necessary to support their arguments. They really impressed me. Twentysomethings with a purpose. Maybe there is hope for America.

I sat with them, speaking of life, and war, and poverty, early into the morning light. And global warming! Do you think Bush will ever admit it's real? Our laughter filled the gardens. They reminded me of my kids; however, I really didn't feel some twenty years older than them. I got the "you're the coolest old dude" comment from Phil. But, that was fair. He held the answer to my most recent prayer – a joint.

After several passes to the left, I explained my travel schedule of the past few days. They understood my need to head back to The Inn. We exchanged hugs and smiles. Chels asked if I'm on MySpace. Of course, I replied. We have to stay in touch. I reached in my bag, pulled out my journal and jotted down my number and MySpace URL: www.myspace.com/misterswiss.

After ripping the page from my book, I handed her my contact info. The name *Luna* caught my eye, now exposed on the next page of the journal.

Meeting those kids was cool. Not necessarily because of our American connection, however that was pleasant. I guess they offered me hope. Hope for our future. Why can't my life be like that back in the States? We're all in such a damn hurry back home. If we just took the time to see the nuances of life, our days would hold so much more meaning.

Walking up the hill in pursuit of sleep, I lit the last cigarette of the night with the last breath of my Bic. I spun around to the waste container I had just passed and launched my shot, with perfect form. Two points! *And the crowd went wild.* My dead Bic was put to rest, a proper burial.

Luna. What a lovely name. With my social calendar filling up so quickly here, I had better make arrangements with her soon. Hopefully she's free Sunday evening. What a way to close out my weekend in the Garden of Eden, sharing Sunday night with a lovely Eve.

After brushing my fangs, I crawled in between the crisp, white sheets of my Holiday Inn bed. Laying there, drifting off to sleep, I felt the touch of an angel. I thanked God for watching over me. I needed it.

My dreams turned to Claire. I still don't like going to bed.

Loneliness always finds me there.

The afternoon heat invaded my room. The slightest slit in the drawn curtains allowed an obnoxious strand of light to hit me directly in the eyes. Good morning, or'a – afternoon, I said to myself. It was 15:07 according to the clock on the nightstand. I have a tough time with European clocks when I first wake up. I have a difficult time with *everything* when I first wake up. I needed coffee. And pain killers. That damn port.

I tossed some water on my face, polished the grill, threw on my New York Yankees cap, and headed for the hotel bar.

As I stepped foot into his establishment, Angelo turned to welcome me back. "*Buon giorno*, my American friend. How are you enjoying this glorious day in paradise?"

My head hurt. I got right down to business. A cappuccino, water, an orange juice, a pack of Marlboro Lights, and some matches. My night was utterly unbelievable, I told him.

"Do we have a hangover this morning? I mean afternoon," he said. "I guess you won't be ordering a whisky chaser for your cappuccino today."

His reference to whisky turned my stomach. Still, his sarcasm was appreciated. He was out of matches. I admitted my guilt as Angelo located a Zippo left behind by another guest. He lit my smoke.

I know I drank a lot last night. But hey, rehab is the new black. I shared with Angelo the treatment I had received at *al Portone*. It was just an amazing night. The caffeine and OJ were beginning to make their way to my brain; I saw a clearing in the fog. I told of the taste treats, the wine and the new friends I'd made in Lugano. But I didn't offer up any information about Colsante's proposition. I can keep a secret.

Especially a secret society kind of secret.

"Sounds like the perfect night in paradise. And what's on tap for today?"

I explained that I was headed to wherever the wind blows. Well, that is once I make my way to the *Piazza della Riforma*. After a long, hot shower, I will be on my way to experience Lugano by day. Finishing my selection of drinks, I asked for a bottle of Coke for takeaway. It's the best thing for a hangover. Ooh, coke. The memory of that vile dandruff of the devil hit me. That *sucks*. I hate it when I cross one of my lines.

As I left for my room, I asked Angelo what the country code is in Switzerland. I had a local number I needed to call, but couldn't remember the Swiss code, 4-something.

"It's 41. Business, or did we meet a heavenly aberration? "

Ah, I get to educate this scholar of the English language. I believe you mean heavenly *apparition*, I told my buddy Angelo.

"Let's hope you're right," he quipped back as I pushed open the door to leave. "May God's love be with you, my brother."

I dialed her number, as I made yet another trek along the lakeshore to the old town district. Refreshed from sleep and a shower, I was prepared to begin my day. I dressed for the evening, even if it was only 17:00. After numerous rings, the call went to voicemail. What a classy girl. Her greeting was recorded in three languages – Italian, French and proper British English. "Hello love, this is Luna. Don't break a girl's heart. Leave me a note."

Her voice was so incredibly sexy; I became as nervous as a school boy while leaving her my message.

Italian Piazzas are one of my passions. They tell the tails of those who came before me. These squares embody the raw spirit of each unique neighborhood – the hub for commerce, news and unity. The backdrop for a community's celebrations of life and of God.

My all-time favorite is *Piazza San Marco* in Venice. The absence of motorized vehicles allows the voice of the masses to be heard above all else, echoing off St. Mark's Basilica to the surrounding marketplace. The Piazza San Marco has the lowest sea-level in Venice. During *Acqua Alta*, the high waters produced by storms in the Adriatic, one has the pleasure of wafting through the knee-high waters that invade the square.

Still, *Piazza della Riforma* was everything I had dreamed of, and more. I entered through a narrow corridor lined with names like Dolce & Gabbana, Gucci, Hugo Boss, and Versace. The clicking of high heels on cobblestone only added to the aura of elegance that is truly the ambiance of Italy. In this case, an extremely Swiss version of Italy.

I stood at the edge of the piazza, absorbing its ambiance, its colors and its life. Lugano's old town square was enchanting. Buildings, dating back centuries, were now home to endless varieties of taste delights. As Sam explained on the Travel Channel, two of the existing *ristoranti*, *Olimpia* and *Federale* were once home to apposing political factions. In 1845, the Olimpia became quarters for the liberal movement of the region. Federale was soon built, right next door, to serve as the drawing-room for a more conservative dogma. These days, they only compete for one another's customers.

I just love living dichotomies. I headed toward the Olimpia for a glass of wine. The perimeter of the piazza was lined with hundreds of chairs, nearly every one taken. Life in Europe holds such warmth and charm. The Europeans live life. They aren't held-up in their homes watching *Reality TV*. They're in the streets living reality.

There, a table with one lone chair, right on the edge of the action. I ordered the waiter's recommended red, reached in my bag to pull out my phone and smokes. My senses were gyrating, all six of them. I needed to capture the marvel of *Piazza della Riforma* in my journal. Taking in the surrounding colors that consumed my world, I reached for the complimentary Olimpia-branded matches standing upright on display in a spotless ashtray. They were wooden, presented in a matchbook, not a box. I enjoy discovering the subtle differences of our ways while traveling. Firing up a smoke, I sat back to enjoy my wine alongside the *piazza*.

*"Lucifer?"*

An old woman, her head wrapped in a ragged brown shawl, looking all homeless, stood directly in front of me. Odd, I didn't think there were homeless people in Switzerland. Still, she looked me squarely in the eyes. I must have misunderstood, God help me.

*"Lucifer!"*

While still holding that smoldering match, my heart sank deep into my bowels. That rat bastard, Silvio. Leave me the hell alone! My rage was preparing its escape from the dungeon of my soul. Just then, the gentleman at the next table leaned toward me and saved Lugano from a vile howl.

"She's asking you for a light. Lucifers means matches." He grinned, "I bet that offers you some relief."

I struck another *lucifer* and lit her cigarette. As she wandered onward, the old lady paused and turned to me.

She smiled and waved.

# chapter twelve

Sa'eed maneuvered his Range Rover along the narrow way that orbited up the steep mountainside overlooking Lugano. The city below glowed bright with life. As we neared the peak of the mountain, I could see an enormous structure peering above the aged stone wall encircling its grounds. An imposing iron gate welcomed us as Sa'eed pushed the button on a remote hanging from his visor. The gate opened and we proceeded through beautifully groomed gardens to the grand entrance of The Mansion.

At first sight, The Mansion's stateliness more reflected that of a Roman palace than a personal residence. Built of marble and stone, it was stunningly beautiful, yet disquieting. Old Uncle Nuncio must have done quite well for himself, I mentioned while still in shock. Colsante assured me that the family had always done well. We exited Sa'eed's ride.

The massive wooden double doors, depicting hand carved images of the *Kama Sutra's* 64 doctrines of pleasure, swung open. We were greeted by the infamous Uncle Nuncio himself, a rather rotund gentleman with a thick Italian accent attached to his English words.

"You must be *Daniele*, the one who possesses the name of the prophet – he who claims the *day of reckoning*. Welcome, my son. I am Nuncio de Sade, but please call me Uncle Nuncio. It is my true pleasure to receive you in my home."

I have always trusted my psychic abilities. Remember, I've had my encounters with the other side. The gift I possess allows me to see the unseen, to feel that which is not there. An old girlfriend of mine actually backed out on buying a house because of that sixth sense of mine. She absolutely loved the place. However, I had that *feeling* as soon as I walked in the door. Not a good feeling. That was all she needed to know. She'd spent enough time with me to trust my instincts. After doing a little internet research, we found there had been a triple homicide-suicide at that address. A young mother of three, just like my girlfriend, murdered her children, then herself. The news article described the crime scene as gruesome and satanic.

There were spirits in The Mansion. I could feel it the moment I passed through the threshold into the spiraling foyer. The bizarre thing, for the first time in my life, I could not discern them as good or evil. But the feeling was overwhelming. Many spirits were living within the confines of Uncle Nuncio's dwelling.

"Colsante, you know the way," Nuncio directed. "Go ahead in and prepare us a cocktail. I'll have a Bombay martini, extra onions this time. Do you know our special guest's poison of choice?"

I asked if he remembered the way I like my vodka. With an affirming nod, Colsante and Sa'eed proceeded down the hall. They knew it was time for their departure. Nuncio put his arm around my shoulder and led me to a small window seat adjacent to the foyer. A bit eerie, this place reminded me of that foreboding mansion in Kubrick's *Eyes Wide Shut*, but with an amazing view of Lugano.

"Daniele, please sit."

We both took our places by the window. A little close quarters for my liking, as Nuncio took up much more than his half. I tend to maintain my personal space with strangers.

"I realize we have just met, but I must tell you – I hold infinite expectations for our association. Colsante and I spoke of you at length this afternoon. He tells me you are a man of honor, one whom we should trust. And I consider one's level of honor to be the truest measure of a man. Trust and honor is what I require. When I receive that which is required, I return the blessing to those who are of the Brotherhood. It is my hope you will do the same."

Ok, not that I would know from firsthand experience, I'm not the frat boy type, but this was sounding like some kind of induction speech prior to my hazing. Hell, I avoided fraternities in college. Why would I want to join one now? Ah, the obvious – money.

"No more talk of these matters until after dinner. It is my honor to offer you the feast of a king this evening. Food is not merely a basic need. Food is a passion."

I'm not good with distinguishing the period of a room's décor, but Nuncio's dining hall furnishings were really old and really big. The widows were covered with rich velvet curtains. The artwork, incredible. Like something straight out of the Vatican's collection.

"Literally. The Brotherhood does have its privileges," Colsante pointed out.

We settled in for the banquet. You'd think this guy Nuncio, with all his cash, would have an army of hotties serving him. That wasn't the case. None of his staff were anywhere even close to Damiano's beauty, Taziana. Maybe my uncle doesn't like the distraction while enjoying *this* passion.

Nuncio obviously loves to eat, based on the spread prepared for only the four of us. The meal was unbelievable, just as promised. *Food, glorious food.* And wine, rare and expensive wine. I would never admit it, but the chef from last night's feast beats Nuncio's hands down. But Nuncio still wins, as his wine list offered the finest vintages from around the globe. I was in *Paradiso*, and three days is not nearly enough time to fully partake of her passions.

My mind raced. This is so *unfuckingbelievable*; some guy from the hills of Appalachia, living the life of the international man of mystery. A toothy grin consumed my face.

I am the magic man.

Dinner was filled with amusing stories of fun times in faraway places. From my experience, the conversation of the extremely wealthy always turns to *the debate*. The debate over who had resided in the most exquisite suite, in the most expensive hotel, in the entire world. But it's all about the level of personal attention one receives, everyone agreed. Asian owned properties seemed to be the choice for that kind of attention. And I thought the Indians did a pretty damn good job of sucking up.

I was quite proud of myself; I held my own in our tales of the travels of the rich and famous. I told them about the time I ran into Jeff Foxworthy in Amsterdam. We were both there on extended stays, taking a timeout on life. We'd meet up for rounds of Heineken at Rookies Coffeeshop, daily. On the third day he finally asked, "You really don't know who I am, do you?" Sure, Jeff. Just Jeff was all I knew; some funny-ass, rich redneck. He finally told me his last name. Hell, I knew that name, but I've never really watched the dude. I might be a redneck if I hadn't intentionally fought to escape it.

My story would have been funnier if they had ever heard of Jeff. I should have told them the one about the time I ran into Bob Hope in a hotel elevator. It was closing time and I was smashed. He was *smasherd*. I said, "Hi Bob! Oops, guess we gotta do a shot." The reply, his body guard all in my face. Apparently, I picked the wrong Bob to joke with. They would have surely known Bob.

Loud talk and laughter filled our evening, until retreating to Nuncio's private chambers. Having covered all the niceties over dinner, Nuncio was ready to get down to business. Which he explained required a cigar and a glass of cognac. I graciously accepted his cognac, presented with unadulterated class, ever so slightly warmed. However, I declined the cigar. They just aren't my kind, I explained. I lit up a Marlboro Light.

His personal chambers, what I would call a library, were fully enclosed by dark, ornate woods and leather. The only exception, a hand carved, gray marble fireplace depicting the fourteen Stations of the Cross. In the center of this holy portrayal, a raging fire. I had to comment on it. I'd never seen anything quite so fascinating. But I really wanted to ask why in the hell he had a fire roaring in the middle of summer. Nuncio must like it toasty.

"I know your brothers have filled you in on our business. More importantly, I must inform you of the quest of our Brotherhood," Nuncio said with definite exactitude, "The service of the *Society* upholds a critical mission."

Sa'eed and Colsante didn't really tell me much about the business side of things. Just that it would afford me freedom, funds and flexibility. All things I truly desire. As Nuncio spoke, I came to learn more about the Society's rich history and its link to the Swiss Guard. What Uncle Nuncio referred to as the Pope's Militia.

In a day of globalization and international alliances, the Brotherhood found it necessary to expand its borders. Rome was never enough, nor was all of Eurasia. Finally the day had come when the Passage could reach all of humankind.

"One could say our society has always existed. Looking at our family lineage, it would appear as such. We are a charitable faction, yet our private business and related mission must always be kept just that – private. Thus, trust and honor are required. Demanded!"

Uncle Nuncio's uncompromising tone served to accentuate his point. He looked me directly in the eyes and in a low voice challenged, "Are you that man? The one we have long anticipated?"

*Am I that man?* Of course Silvio's words haunted me. Before meeting him, that would have been an easy dilemma to resolve. No longer was it so simple. But who am I to fight the Universe? I recalled Silvio's wisdom. *Good and evil can be very deceiving.* I mean, come on. Maybe he's right. Is there truly an absolute truth?

Uncle Nuncio continued, "Inscrutable secrets, handed down over the centuries, are held by the Brotherhood. Even within the Society, only a select few fully hold the *truth.* I will solve for you the enigma of our universe, if you are that man."

I was more than a little spooked, folks. Nuncio had already told me way too much. He'd already taken me in like family, entrusting me with sacred secrets. All things considered, I've inherited the bloodline of the Brotherhood. I must trust the Universe to guide me to my *grand destiny.* Otherwise, I may not see the light of a new day.

"Are you the one? The enigma is waiting to be unraveled before your eyes. Daniele, your course has been plotted. Accept the role of leadership that awaits you. I ask you one final time. – Are you that man?"

Curiosity. Plain and simple, my curiosity cradled my demise. I was crazed. I must see the enigma disentangle. Me, holding the secrets of the universe, I fantasized. Knowledge is power. I always knew I was chosen to do great things. Today, I embark on that new life.

I took a stand, emphatically stating, "I am that man."

Nuncio replied, "I have a test for you. You *must* answer correctly. We shall then place our trust in you as *the one*. Answering incorrectly would be blasphemous! My question is simple. When you close your eyes, what do you see?"

His question was odd on many levels. On the surface, one would immediately want to answer *nothing*. But I explained to my uncle, that had never been the case for me. For as long as I can remember, I have seen visions when I close my eyes. Not that they necessarily gave me miraculous insights. Sometimes they would, but usually I just see faces. Faces that morph into other faces, and then still to others. At times, they are evil and at times they are good. Too, I can look deep into their eyes, the windows to their souls.

Uncle Nuncio stood at attention and announced, "We are in the presence of the anointed one!"

It was a celebration. A celebration for what, I wasn't exactly sure. But, obviously I gave the correct answer. More cognac was offered and poured. It was a toast. A moment of great honor for all to treasure, for all eternity. Nuncio sat back down in his overstuffed leather chair and directed me to do the same.

He leaned progressively closer as he offered me the key, the answer to the secrets of our universe.

"The next seven years are pivotal for the world as we know it. Over these coming years, we will face many battles. However, our personal struggles will serve to establish what the *new evolution* is to become. We will be like gods on that dawning day. It is up to us, up to you, to see that our Brotherhood not only survives, but possesses the new heavens and earth – as it was always meant to be."

As he continued, I became enlightened. Gaining more knowledge and insight than which was spoken. The spirits within The Mansion seemed to pass through me. I seized their wisdom, as my uncle shared the secrets of the Brotherhood.

"Over the course of time, the Brotherhood of the Passage has been entrusted with the knowledge of the coming. Others have held the truth throughout this period of Creation, but they were incapable of fulfilling their mission. Thus, their civilizations were destroyed as punishment for their failure. The Brotherhood has never failed. Will never fail! Thus, we have been entrusted to hold the truth to this day. The key to the enigma is this, 12212012."

12212012? That number made no sense to me, whatsoever.

"You see, Daniele, there are spiritual warriors within our sect, currently numbering 1110. It saddens me to say, we have recently lost a brother to the other side. He failed us, but you are the one. Again, because of you, there is balance in our universe. You are number 1111."

He kept throwing numbers at me. Not my strong suit. But 1111 was familiar, frighteningly familiar. I see that number everywhere, all the time. On clocks, cash register receipts, street addresses, and even the first internet password assigned to me was a variation of that number. Numerologists have long consider 1111 an aberratious phenomenon. Events linked to the time 11:11 and the number 1111 appear in life more frequently than can be explained by mere mathematical chance or coincidence. I first learned of 1111 in my studies of Carl Jung's teachings on Synchronicity.

What a coincidence!

Some people believe 1111 is an auspicious sign, while others view it as an indication of the presence of a spirit. For me, 1111 is just one more example of the freaky shit that seems to come my way. – Yet, this doesn't explain 12212012.

Uncle Nuncio continued, "12212012. The end of the heavens and earth, the *passage* to our New Creation. The Mayan civilization once held the secret. But they were foolish. They exposed our secret to the world, thus ruined for their lack of discretion. Regardless, the enigma is revealed by the end of the Mayan calendar. December 21$^{st}$, 2012. The end of the 13th b'ak'tun. An era of destruction. An age of re-birth. You see, my son, this is not the first cycle of Creation. We are actually living in the fourth Creation of the heavens and earth. During the first three, the spiritual authorities battled and failed. Now in the end times of this fourth world, we must prepare for the fifth and final passage. Our domain to conquer!"

I knew that number – 12212012. I knew it as December 21, 2012. Freak me out! Ready for another coincidence? I came upon this date while researching 1111. Strange as it may seem, according to the Mayan race, the transition from our current Creation into the next will occur at the onset of the Winter Solstice in 2012. Which is on December 21, 2012. The exact time of that solstice, 11:11.

The other details of our conversation held little relevance at this point, given the magnitude of 12212012. But there were many more truths shared that evening. But I have already said too much.

As the hour neared midnight, Uncle Nuncio rushed our conversation for the first time all evening.

"We will meet at Banque UniSuisse first thing Monday morning, say 11:00. Sa'eed, be sure the Director's Room in the penthouse is available for us. We will need to open Daniele a Numbered Account and please see that he receives his Centurion Card as soon as humanly possible. Our prodigy will require the spending power of the Amex Black Card."

I wanted to ask about salary, but learned that all my needs would be met by the *family*. Nuncio explained there were many privileges to being of the bloodline of original land owners. One very beneficial advantage, the family is free from the obligation of Swiss tax. Therefore, all my expenses would be managed through family accounts.

"You see, my son, you have received your inheritance. One of endless wealth and power. You know what that means?"

Girls! I knew the answer to that question.

He smiled and winked at Sa'eed and Colsante. We laughed for the first time since entering Nuncio's chambers.

"We are approaching the end of the final hour," our uncle announced. "Shall we proceed to the garden for this evening's *fête*?"

We shuffled out the door and down a seemingly endless corridor, with each of our footsteps echoing in cadence. *To the garden for the fête?* How *chic* a way of life I now lead.

Excusing himself, Nuncio assured, "I will be with you shortly. I must attend to a few details in preparation for the evening's celebration. Daniele, tonight we honor you, the man."

I didn't believe he was trying to be cool – *you da' man*. But why, all of a sudden, did I feel like a sheep being led to slaughter? A very real sense of terror shot through my bones. If I live to see the morning, I will be the king. And if I don't, it may be all for the better.

Sa'eed led me to the *baths*. That's what he called it. Locker room would be a more American term. Except I've never before stood in a locker room of marble and solid gold. Pedestals, with hooks placed above, lined the walls to replace the standard gray grated lockers. No thief would dare penetrate these depths of The

Mansion. I was told to shower before entering the garden. It's part of family etiquette. I placed my things on a pedestal and went for a *douche*.

Upon returning to my selected pedestal, I found a plush white towel and a white silk robe resting atop, perfectly presented with a single orchid as an accent. What bothered me was my phone and passport were gone. The rest of my stuff doesn't matter, but I always keep those two items on my person when abroad. You gotta stay connected and you gotta be able to *get out*.

Sa'eed assured me that my things were only a request away. "Daniel, don't you get it? This is your new life. You are in total control of your destiny."

We exited yet another set of double doors, which led to the garden. Passing through to the other side, I had to take a moment to suck up the sights and sounds. The music was exhilarating, a requiem of chant and melody. Sculptured hedges and literally hundreds of varieties of flowering plants surrounded the pool, which was flooded by a lighted waterfall. Enormous trees, as old as the earth, stood tall to create an umbrella of green. The only distraction from the loveliness of Uncle Nuncio's garden was the divinity of the G*irls of the Passage*.

I had entered the true *Garden of Eden*.

Surrounding the pool was every imaginable variation of beauty one could ever desire, each fully disrobed. Girls from all regions of the world, in every delectable color and shape. My head throbbed as I took in this erotic scene. With great discretion, I inquire of Sa'eed, "Are they prostitutes?"

"We would never call our girls by such a term. But they are here to meet your every need, my sovereign one. The choice is yours. Select one, or as many as you like. Once you have chosen your delight, the rest of us will step forward to satisfy the needs of your discarded lovers."

I no longer feared death.

I feared my new life.

The whole *paying for it* thing never appealed to me. That's a line I will never cross. I so much more enjoy the chase, the romancing, and the conquest. If I don't earn it, I don't want it. Why would I pretend when it comes to the most intimate aspect of life?

Colsante offered the suggestion that I select an enhancer. He noted the wait staff could fulfill my every dietary requirement. I just needed a cocktail. I turned to the Swedish beauty that had been towering next to me. One of the few still dressed for the occasion. I requested a Ketel One, tonic, lemon – short.

"Yes my Lord, I will bring the beverage of your choosing. May I offer you an essence to *strengthen* the evening's experience?"

I declined. Only a dead man would need Viagra at a time like this. My focus turned to the dark haired, dark eyed *goddess* on the far side of the pool. She looked *fine*. Tall, lean and breasts the size of peaches. Oh, so perfect. It struck me, she's a Claire.

The gentlemen stood around in their robes awaiting my move. Maybe this is a common occurrence among the Euro-crowd I'm hangin' with, but for this American – *oh, bebe, hot, hot, hot*! Just then I realized that my underwear had gone the way of my passport. Nothing was holding me back. There was only a silk robe between me and my chosen one across the water. I struggled. I can't cross that line, but she's so perfect.

Uncle Nuncio stepped forward and greeted the congregation. "Tonight is the night we have awaited – *the night on high*. It is my honor to humbly offer you Daniele, the man who will lead us to the new evolution."

Pretty cool being the guest of honor, yet exhausting. I don't like so much attention, especially when people are thinking more of me than what's true. The men all shook my hand and the girls hugged and kissed me. Those were some amazing hugs. My *goddess* was the last in line. After an intense embrace, she began to step away. I reached out and gently took her hand. She smiled sweetly, proudly taking her place by my side.

"Let's get this party started," Uncle Nuncio proclaimed.

This time, trying to be cool.

The lights dimmed to the glow of torches placed throughout the garden. The pulse of the music grew stronger, faster and louder, filling the warm midnight air.

Monique was my ideal. Beautiful, charming and a crazy sense of humor. I made a wise choice. She was great! Her hometown was *Villefranche-sur-Mer*, a quaint old world village situated on the Mediterranean in the South of France. She briefly lived in Paris, but found it to be such a bore. The Parisians are too uptight for her. Besides, she loved the simple elegance of life in Lugano. It reminded her of home.

We had so much in common. I told her I had savored the delights of her hometown many times before. I adore the South of France. And *Villefranche-sur-Mer* was by far my favorite destination in the region. I recalled this little café along the waterside that I so loved to visit. Partially because of a cutie that worked there. – At the exact same moment, we both lost it. She was *that girl*. Best of all, she remembered me! What are the chances?

"I thought you were pretty cool for an older gentleman," she shared.

Monique and I danced to a dimly lit, secluded corner of the garden. She softly kissed my face as we moved to the music swirling around our bodies. I caressed her gently, as she aggressively pulled me ever closer. My head was spinning out of control. I was in the arms of an angel. A very devilish angel.

We embraced and kissed as the music penetrated my thoughts. She softly mouthed each word of the song echoing around us, with every seductive intention.

Lovers throughout the garden were already enjoying their sport. The moans of lust filled the air. My heart was pounding, my spirit weak. Monique whispered, "Come. You are free to do with me whatever your heart desires. I am here to serve you. Our lives were destined to converge, yet again. *Consume me.*"

My head was dizzy and my mouth was dry.

# 13

Having finally made my way back to Paradiso, I stepped into the Holiday Inn bar. Wishing Angelo good morning, I had to ask if he actually lived behind that counter. Smiling, he concurred, he really didn't have much of a personal life.

I asked for a beer.

"It's 7:00 in the morning," he replied.

Scotch, I countered. But he didn't get it. I'm glad, he grabbed me the beer. I don't even like scotch, especially at 7:00 in the morning.

I know. You're waiting to hear what happened. Believe me, it's worth the wait. Just give me a minute. First, I believe the knowledge gained on that *morning after* is significant in trying to make sense of this insane night of sinful desire.

I needed information, background. I needed to find someone in this town that could give me insight into the Brotherhood of the Passage. I needed to perform a little corporate espionage. I seriously had no clue as to what I'd just lived through. Even, worse, what I'd just gotten myself into. So I decided to start with the man in front of me. Without giving up any secrets, I ask Angelo if the number 12212012 meant anything to him.

Angelo's face twisted in a knot. He replied, "Where'd you say you were last night?"

I hadn't said. You know, secrets and all. But his query indicated some familiarity, or possibly concern.

"There is a great deal of legend wrapped around that number. A number that is better not to hold in one's mind. Why do you ask? Were you offered this number last night?"

His portrayal of the number, coated in curiosity, offered me no insight. He certainly wasn't giving up any secrets. Then I thought, could it be that Angelo is one of us? A brother? Possibly, he's protecting the secret just as I am. If he were a member of the Passage, he's obviously beneath the ranks of the elite. He knew of the number, but believed it better not to be known. Only those of us *on high* are permitted to possess the full truth. Uncle Nuncio made that absolutely clear.

It was my turn to pose an inquiry. "Could it be that you and I are brothers, Angelo?"

His smile lit up the room, "We are brothers!"

That's the sign I'd been seeking. But, is my commitment to the Brotherhood one I could live with? As if I had a choice. I needed to know more; but, it really didn't matter. I shook hands at The Mansion. I toasted. I made it known, *I am that man.* Besides, I wasn't going anywhere. At least not out of the country. My passport was safely locked away in the *trusted* hands of the Brotherhood of the Passage.

Angelo interrupted my thoughts. "I had serious concerns for you, my brother. I thank God you have seen the light!"

I thought it strange he spoke of God, while I considered the Brotherhood more closely aligned with Satan's camp. But as they say, good and evil can be very deceiving.

I finished up my beer and told Angelo I really needed to get some sleep. So much has happened over the past few days. I was completely exhausted. I asked for another beer to take to my room. I also needed smokes and some matches. They had my brand, but were still out of fire. I grabbed my stuff and headed toward the door.

Angelo stopped me for a parting remark. "My brother, be very careful. Evil can be very deceiving. Please keep this message in your thoughts today."

He then quoted Ecclesiastes 3:16-18

> Moreover I saw under the sun that in the place of justice, wickedness was there, and in the place of righteousness, wickedness was there as well. I said in my heart, God will judge the righteous and the wicked, for he has appointed a time for every matter, and for every work. I said in my heart with regard to human beings that God is testing them to show that they are but animals.

"Remember, *you* my brother, you are more than an animal. And no one knows the exact time of the reckoning, but God."

Turning to him, I said, "May God's love be with you, bro."

Angelo's smile returned.

I went to my room, popped open the beer and lit a smoke with my last match. I wondered if Angelo and I were talking about the same brotherhood. I must trust the Universe to direct me, I deliberated. Sitting there, on the edge of my bed, I looked out the window to a tranquil Lugano morning.

I prayed.

*Lord, my God.*
*I think I am lost.*
*Please send help.*
*In Jesus' name,*
*Amen.*

It was 8:20 a.m. I set my phone for a 4:20 p.m. wake up. Tonight is the big night! I crawled into bed.

Alone.

Ok, so where was I? The Mansion, Monique and that Enigma tune, *The Principles of Lust*, still playing in my head. That song has always left me with an uneasy feeling. But I like it, nonetheless.

The words continued to loft through my mind.

Lust absorbed my soul. Monique desired my passion. Her words were, *consume me*, as she loosened the belt tied around my waist. I bet she says that to all the guys. Still, *consume* her. There was nothing I desired more at that very minute. But, my head was dizzy and my mouth was dry.

I told Monique I needed another drink, and asked what she would like. She showed me, pulling me toward a lounge yet to be occupied by the other lovers baring their souls. Her touch made me quiver. The gentle pull of her hand drew me ever closer, to a position of dominance rising above my lover.

"I will quench your thirst from the sweat of my body," she sighed before running her tongue slowly from my chest up to the narrows of my neck.

She trapped me with desire. My passion prepared for its initial assault. Monique placed me seductively close, then pulled away to

162

extend our shared temptation a moment longer. Her lips were moist, dripping, like that of a tiger prepared to take its kill. She closed her eyes, tilting her head back, as if prepared to cry out in agony. I was armed, primed, on target. Heaven was on its way.

As I gradually urged my way forward, my *Girl of the Passage* lying beneath me quietly vowed, "You are the Son of the World, my morning star. Hurt me. Punish me. Chastise me with your might, my Lord."

I couldn't do it. I just couldn't. I am *not* that guy. And Monique was no longer that sweet, innocent girl I once knew from *Villefranche-sur-Mer.* I don't do prostitutes and I don't want to be the Son of the World! Even if I wasn't paying for her myself, it's still an evil I couldn't be party to. I was scared. I couldn't show my lack of appreciation to my host. But, I could not accept his gift. I wanted out.

I had failed Uncle Nuncio.

I left that luscious demon lying on her back, unfulfilled, rejected and pissed. I headed for the baths. I needed to get my things and get the hell out! I'd spent my night dancing with evil and now I wished to take it all back. How in the world can I back out, now? I've made a deal with the devil. I knew that truth deep within my soul.

Approaching the entrance of the baths, Uncle Nuncio appeared seemingly out of nowhere.

"Where are you going, my son? Are the Girls of the Passage not good enough for our honored one?" His words showed grave concern.

I insisted that each one is as lovely as the next, in their own blessed way. That was not the issue. I had taken on an uneasy stomach, I negotiated. Maybe it was too much of a good thing at dinner.

"We have prepared your quarters. Perhaps you would appreciate a rest. I will have a guide take you there."

My quarters?

"Yes, didn't Colsante tell you? This is your kingdom, my child. You hold the keys to the castle. I will have your darling Monique bring you a seltzer. That should help ease your pain."

At the moment, I wasn't interested in Monique, seltzer or my quarters. I wanted to get the fuck off the top of this mountain. I asked where Colsante and Sa'eed had headed off to.

"Oh, they had to go. Sa'eed received a call from his wife. The baby was getting fussy and so was his mother-in-law. He just had a son, you know? What a little prince."

I was on my own, with Uncle Nuncio standing between me and freedom. I tried another approach. A quiet walk in the night air was all I needed. I'll just grab my things and check my messages, while clearing my head.

I explained he must realize, this evening had been more than a little overwhelming. I was not prepared for such an honor to be bestowed upon me. He seemed to buy it. My uncle directed a servant to immediately have my clothes brought to the baths.

"A walk in the garden is precisely what you need. I love passing through our family's final resting place at night. It gives one a very real sense of the finality of this world. Alone in the garden, where no one can disturb you. You can find your rest there."

And where no one can hear my screams, I considered.

I entered the double doors of the baths, finding my clothes pressed and folded on my pedestal. I hadn't even considered that the baths were coed, until a perky little Asian hottie scooted past without a stitch of hair on her body. Checking her out, I grabbed my mobile to see if I'd missed any calls. Not one. And I was hoping to hear from Luna. I laughed at myself – that one-track mind of mine. Just what I need, another woman to cause me trouble; or maybe it's the other way around.

I finished getting dressed and did a final check of my possessions before departing. I reached inside my jacket pocket to assure my passport was ready for us to move on. It wasn't there. I quickly turned, as I felt a presence behind me. Nuncio was standing there, his arms crossed. I grilled him about my passport. I don't mess around when it comes to my freedom. He assured me there was no reason to be alarmed. Sa'eed simply needed my documentation for the arrangement of my accounts.

"Now if you will excuse me, I must retire. I have business in Rome tomorrow. We will consummate the details of your service on Monday – 11:00, sharp. Enjoy the first day of the rest of your life, my one," Uncle Nuncio said with deliberate significance.

I was feeling trapped. Not just in The Mansion, but this town. Hell, this country. No frickin' passport. Just great.

Escaping the crowds, I moved deeper into the garden. The grounds were eerily beautiful at night, lit by the stars and moon. I kinda dig old graveyards, so I made my way to the family's final resting place. I pondered if Nuncio knew. If he knew I was having doubts. If he did, I may soon be wearing a dead man's rope. Of that I'm sure. I questioned, is that why he so freely sent me off to the *final resting place?*

Standing at the ornate iron gate of the cemetery, I paused. I'm goin' in. Like I said before, it just might be better if I don't live to see the light of a new day.

I have never seen such an elaborate cemetery. The enormous headstones were each unique, showing great care to portray the stature of the person it represented. Yet, others were discretely simple. Odd symbols topped every marker, but not one cross in the place. I've never seen such a curious final resting place in all my late night grave tours.

Terror stroked my flesh as I rushed passed a freshly covered grave. Still alive, I had to find a way out. Scanning my environment, I located another gated passageway on the far perimeter of the cemetery. Fueled by fear, I went into a mad dash toward the exit. I made my escape climbing up and over the gate. I was free, still breathing, my heart pounding.

As I followed the path downward, my sin grew real. I had made a deal with the devil. Although, I had yet to officially consummate it, I still possessed the *secret*. I was bonded to the Brotherhood. How had it come to this? I truly am a good man, with a big heart. Maybe, too big at times. Regardless, I have betrayed God. For what? Power? Wealth? Women?

My agony grew stronger. I searched my mind for a Bible verse, an effort to appeal to God. Matthew 4:1 came to mind. That passage I used while debating the devil with my work buddy Joe.

> Then Jesus was led by the Spirit into the wilderness
> to be tempted by the devil.

God's own Spirit led Him into the wilds to be tempted? Could it be that this is part of God's will for me, I prayed. I guess we all have to tread through the fire at times. To strengthen and to purify. Jesus can at least understand my predicament. He's gone His rounds with the devil. It's just that He held up under pressure so much better than me. Jesus came out sinless. I have not.

It was almost 6:30 in the morning when I reached the city proper. My phone began to vibrate. Who in the hell would be calling me at this hour? It indicated a blocked number. Ah, it's still Saturday night in Columbus. It's probably just Jenny Jarvis drunk dialing me. That girl is such a trip. I answered with my standard, *hey girl, what's up?*

The voice on the other end of the line was not that of Jenny Jarvis. However, this voice was familiar to me, in three different languages. It was Luna.

"I'm so glad I caught you. You said in your message that you're a night person who enjoys the sunrise of a new day. I thought I'd test you, just to see if you would tell a girl the truth."

She was even more charming in real time. My curiosity was heightened. I didn't even think to ask Silvio what she looked like. He called her an amazing creation. That was good enough for me. We made arrangement to meet for dinner at a roadhouse in her village, just a few kilometers south of Paradiso. Her favorite little grotto. She promised the perfect evening waited us.

My Nokia alerted me it was time to start the new day. 4:20 p.m. The perfect way to start my day. I shuffled through my things covering the standard issue Holiday Inn desk and located a book of matches. I lit a smoke. My scavenger hunt revealed Karim's number. I dialed him. I was going to need a ride to the south side of the lake in a few hours.

The Universe is definitely guiding me. I trusted that. I have always found my way through life's riddles. I'll try to just put it out of my mind for now. It's probably better if I let my subconscious mind work out the details without my involvement.

I'll make sense of this chaos when I arrive at the bank first thing tomorrow morning. 11:00, sharp.

But tonight, I have a date with an amazing creation.

# chapter fourteen

The scent of the world's finest leather filled Karim's Mercedes.
Lounging in the rear seat of his taxi, I felt as if I had seized the
universe. The past three weeks had been an endless line of
Mercedes S-Classes, driver included. Now I find myself in the
position to lead this life of luxury, forever.

My thoughts turned to Luna as the sweet aroma of leather invaded
my senses, like an aphrodisiac, inducing every nerve in my body
to tingle. I finally get to meet her, my luscious temptress. I
fantasized about her beauty and her charms. I recalled that lovely,
soft voice I heard over the phone. Her laugh was coy, yet sexy.
Yeah, yeah, I know. I'm a romantic. But, after last night's devilish
nymphs, a nice girl to subdue would be righteous.

"You will truly enjoy the grotto she has chosen. It's situated on
the southernmost shoreline," Karim explained. "I should hope she

has arranged for an outdoor table. This evening's weather is ideal for dining alongside Lake Lugano, as you taunt tonight's icon."

I laughed at his description – an icon. So true. Women are to be worshipped, I added. There is always something uniquely striking about every *fem* I encounter. Karim could relate. We began to expose our views on life and love. Including the places each had taken us. We spoke of our past romances, and their imminent demise. Somehow, even amidst the translation of languages and cultures, we truly understand one another.

Our destination was *Riva San Vitale*, a small village about 10 kilometers opposite Lugano. Cruising along the winding lakeshore highway to our destination, Karim suddenly yanked the steering wheel to a hard left, throwing us into an immediate drift. The force of his maneuver slung me across the backseat, landing my body against the opposite door. Reversing the wheel with precision, he corrected our spin and gunned us away from the scene of the crime.

"I apologize for the abruptness of our change in direction. It appeared we had a roadblock ahead. They're probably looking for some foreign thief escaping to the border with his net. You'll have that. So, trust me to reroute our trip to Luna," Karim said calmly. "I know a back way, always. I won't allow you to be late, my American brother."

Karim was one kick-ass driver. He increased the pace of our previously leisurely ride, speeding away from Interpol over the ancient Roman back roads of the Alps. At this rate, I was sure to be on time for my date. One should never allow an angel to wait.

Karim's reaction to the *polizia* was performed with skilled exactness, almost natural, or possibly highly trained. I pondered; does my Iraqi friend have something to hide? I had to ask. I'm anything but shy.

He explained that life had made it necessary for him to become familiar with *ways around*. His statement led me to think I may have aligned myself with the wrong colleague until he assured me there was nothing evil about his circumstances.

"I'm not a terrorist, if that's what you're thinking. It's just that I have no passport, no papers. It's a long story, but the inspection that awaited us would have caused you to be late. Late, because of me."

I thanked him for his consideration. That Karim is such a nice guy, *for a terrorist*. I told him I totally understood. The no passport thing is a real pain in the ass. I explained that via unfortunate circumstances, I too was without a passport until Monday. We laughed at what odd allies we made; two opposing foreign factions, now fugitives, fleeing Interpol.

"Speaking of, I have quite the challenge ahead. I must leave tomorrow for a trip to Spain," Karim continued. "Under the circumstance, I must drive the back way around, avoiding manned border crossings and the *polizia*. But no worries, my friend. I promised you a ride to the airport in the morning. I'll leave Lugano once I've fulfilled my commitment to you."

The airport, well there's been a change in plans. I actually needed to be picked up a little earlier. I have a meeting at Banque UniSuisse at 11:00, sharp. My passport will be awaiting me there, I explained.

"It sounds like you don't know where you're going," Karim joked.

He was probably right. But I'll deal with that tomorrow. I settled back in my seat, now that all the excitement was over, and chilled my thoughts in preparation for Luna.

Dust arose as Karim's taxi made the wide turn around the dirt drive that encircled a grassy island, hosting a single brushy tree that shaded the entrance of the restaurant. It was a mostly open air café, so lovely and so *Italiano*.

"I'll see you at the Holiday Inn in the morning, or possibly you will call for a ride from this side of the lake. You have my number in your phone? Call me if you need anything, buddy – day or night. We're friends, remember."

As Karim pulled away, the proprietor, all ninety-five pounds of him, recognized me without a word. I was obviously expected.

"Welcome you, the Americano," he said in limited English. "You sit here," he directed while taking my arm, leading me to the table. Ooh, tonight you come to view the *bella*," he whispered with a song in his voice. "You a happy man. The Luna is what you Americano *sayz* hot!"

He was a bit of an entertainer. I like that. You gotta have fun in life. The evening was off to a great start. Our table, complete with white linens and fresh cut flowers, was secluded under the branches of a tree nestled alongside the lake. Nothing more romantic was imaginable. He gave us his best. The mood was set. The music, a violin piece evoking a painful passion, only heightened my arousal. Luna, I repeated in my head. What a captivating name. I hadn't even seen her and was already in lust.

Across the patio appeared a goddess, approaching with her eyes affixed on only me. She wore a silk wrap skirt that flowed freely in the breeze, pulling gently at its seam to expose her long, slender legs. A tiny black top formed itself tightly around her torso, accentuating her perfectly perky breasts. Glistening in the setting sun, her rich brown hair tossed to and fro as she moved closer. She was stunning, an apparition. *An amazing creation.* She had to be Luna.

"Daniel, I've been awaiting this moment," she confidently said while reaching out to me.

Kissing that lovely hand, her sweet aroma attached itself to my lips. I breathed her in. She was exquisite, alluring, possessing just the right touch of androgyny. I was immediately taken by her beauty. Soon, too, by her mesmerizing charm. Luna's free-spirited style excited me. We were familiar souls, relating. Possibly long lost lovers, reunited after an agonizing separation? We just clicked. We shared similar taste in music, art and were both of the more open-minded persuasion. Most entrancing, Luna and I shared *a chemistry*. That was unmistakable the moment we first touched.

While the evening turned to night, we shared our dreams, our desires and our pasts. Luna's beautiful eyes filled with tears as she lamented over the heartbreaking death of her first and only true love. "One of life's unpredictable tragedies," she sighed. "But that was so long ago," she said with a sad smile.

I found myself caring, wanting to help, to fix her. She quickly regained her composure, while gently ran her fingers along the veins of my wrist to the palm of my hand. The sensation traced through every nerve in my body. Her seductive ways were invigorating. Anticipation flooded my flesh.

Our host approached to present his best bottle of champagne, if it would be our pleasure to indulge. Luna immediately accepted, and then explained to me this evening's pleasures were a gift from our mutual ally, Silvio. We celebrated. Luna couldn't imagine me leaving *Paradiso*. Not without her, she teased.

"Silvio told me I was sure to find you exciting. But, I had no idea just how much. You offer me a light I have not seen for so long. I need, tonight, to be with you." She toyed with me. Reached out to me, we embraced. We kissed.

I knew in my heart, this seductive bond was purely a physical kind of chemistry. Not as it was with Claire. This was not love at first sight. Yet once again, it was merely pleasure.

❧❧

Priceless pleasure. I was left paralyzed, yet visibly trembling. A haze of Nag Champa filled her bedroom. The arms of that burning incense wrapped around our naked bodies, attaching itself to our moist skin. Her oils dripped from my lips. The music inebriated my spirit. Luna had habituated my flesh, and I, hers.

When one is in the presence of a seductive angel, new heights of passion can be attained. We did, and she wanted more. I'm not a man who would ever refuse to satisfy the carnal desires of my companion. I gasped for oxygen, while bleeding sweat from our first encounter. But hell, what did I expect. She's half my age.

Luna had completely mesmerized me. It started with a full body massage enhanced with oils she had selected on a recent trip to the Far East. Those oils, which had now found their way to my tongue, offered the unexpected taste of sweet, forbidden fruit.

What a paradise, this Eden.

She left me for but a moment. Tea was required for us to regain our strength. She promised, these particular leaves were unlike any others. A special blend gifted her by a stranger met on that recent Orient escapade.

Luna returned with a tray, hosting Asian tea essentials. While the pot steeped, we sat face to face, our beings fully exposed. The shadows cast by a candle's flicker drew me into a dream state. My body was relaxed, satisfied. Luna turned away to pour her brew. I ran my fingers down her long, lean back. That simple touch heightened my desire, my thirst.

The tea was extraordinary. Naturally sweet, with a bite at the finish. However, its harsh aroma filled her room. I felt high. I could fall for this girl. She lived life to the extreme. She lived for experience. And she admired those same qualities in me.

After another steamy sip, I leaned forward to kiss her puffy lips. Brushing aside her hair to fully expose her splendor, I gradually ran my fingers across her cheek. Reaching her slightly extended tongue, she kissed my finger tips. I caressed her breast, gently stroking her protruding nipples. Luna exhaled with a tortured moan. It was my turn to indulge my lover.

Our fire once again ignited. Our bodies became entangled. Her skin was tight, supple. I massaged her body and caressed her every curve. I tasted her passion and felt her deeply. Luna cried out in untainted ecstasy, being fully served by her devoted love slave.

Upon fulfillment, Luna quietly regained her poise. Then she suddenly turned, pinning me to the mattress while aggressively asserting, "You are a god. The keeper. What is it that you possess? I must know. Promise me you will stay. This is your destiny. You can never leave."

I'm really not that amazing, but tonight I'd outdone myself. In all honesty, my power of attraction, and my performance, was pretty damn impressive. I was feeling like the king, yet again. A very drunk king. *Too drunk!*

A swirling roar filled the air, forcing me headfirst into a spin. Intensity of sight and sound stretched my mind. This was more than an alcohol induced distortion. – I'm hallucinating. Drugged? Trippin'! Like a pebble dropped into a pond, Luna's words visually rippled throughout the darkening room. I was overtaken by psychedelic colors and liquid lights. Voices, laughter and screams echoed throughout her domain. Like a puddle of melted wax, my body sank deep into her sheets.

Luna wiped the perspiration from my forehead with her silk panties, which had made their way to my pillow. Maintaining her position of dominance, she began to sing. Her voice so sweet, her words so tormenting.

*Shut your eyes and relax*
*So sweet a pleasure awaits you*
*Under my touch you have no control*
*This act of passion I bestow upon you...*

Accepting my mental state, I surrendered, sprawled back to enjoy the ride. It's best to just go with these sort of things. A comfortable numbness cradled me. Luna grasped me, straddled me – overpowered me. My eyes, wide shut in anticipation of imminent pleasure.

Dreaming, eyes wide open, from this nightmare there was no escape. Claire? It was Claire atop of me. I saw her eyes, I heard her voice. I felt her touch. That memorable fit. I could taste her desire. My lips struggled for just one more kiss. Those pouty lips poured over me, moist and sweet. I hurt. I knew it was only temporary. I knew this was only a vision. Yet, I felt alive. I felt real. I felt love. I *felt!* I cried out, "Oh, God! I loved. Why the promise? Only to die."

The love.

The evil.

I heard its voices cry out. Immediately, I was alone. Claire had once again been stolen from me. Anguish stole all joy from my flesh. Luna's room melted – shrinking claustrophobically close to the bed where I was laid, powerless to this living nightmare. The smell of rancid death embalmed the air. I was trapped.

Restrained.

His voice surrounded her chambers with an empty, echoing tenor. I tightened the grip the lids held over my eyes. My heart pounded, intensely, loudly.

*Your path has been plotted. Your destiny determined.*
*Now your crowning completed. You are he, the one. You*
*see my son, the bag is not empty. It holds all I have*
*promised you. All you have experienced. All you desired.*
*It is all from me. The bag is now yours to carry, for all*
*eternity.*

Out of absolute terror, I struggled to fight my way free. The
forces that controlled me had to be stopped. My eyes shot open. I
gathered my sight. There, straddling me where Claire once rested
was that all too familiar a smile, presented with a nearly complete
set of teeth. Silvio.

I gasped for air.

Awakened by my own ghastly shriek, I found Luna wrapped in a
towel, still dripping from a hot shower. The steam moistened air
still possessing the stench of stale sex lofted around her room like
a disgusting LA smog.

"Daniel, it was a lovely evening. But it's getting late. I do have a
full schedule tomorrow. I certainly hope we can do this again
sometime. You have my number, no?"

She was throwing me out? After the night we just fucking shared?
Our night of perfect passion. I was starting to fall for this girl!
Totally freaked, I found my clothes. Her tone puzzled me. It was
almost business-like. We'd just experienced the most incredible
night of sex and Luna was treating me like a client!

"Oh, and *Dan*, no worries about the issue of money. Tonight is
compliments of your buddy Silvio. He certainly is impressed with
you. Now I know why." She flashed me an iniquitous smile. "It
was a lovely evening. So much so, I may be calling you."

She laughed with a filth that sickened my soul. I felt my stomach turn to fire. Tonight, I unknowingly crossed that line. Deception had filled my life. Evil had overrun my world.

Anguish had become my anchor.

Tonight, Lucifer crowned me with my destiny.

# chapter fifteen

I was a man possessed. Beaten down to the very limits of my humanity. My life had turned black, one bad decision after another. Hurting and being hurt. Living among the lost. It was time I came to terms with the truth. – Evil lives in me.

I am evil personified.

The Son of Lucifer.

I faced a nightlong hike back to Holiday Inn Hell. The path awaiting me, my indoctrination, a journey through that fiery place where there is weeping and gnashing of teeth. The raw revelation of my cancerous evils oozed from my every lymph node. I mourned the passing of my soul as I walked through the valley of the shadow of death, which led me beside the still waters of Lake Lugano, on the path to Paradiso. My personal hell. I didn't know what to do. I was lost. Spiritually lost. I had betrayed God with my life, my words and my actions. I could never approach Him again. For tonight, I had been crowned as King of the Brotherhood of *Satan*.

Clouds filled the sky, preventing any light to shine down from above. I was frightened of the evils in this world. I was frightened of myself. I needed comfort, but it was too late. The Universe had already bestowed upon me an everlasting curse. I cried out to God, but He wasn't answering.

I mouthed the words of the first Bible verse I memorized as a child.

The 23$^{rd}$ Psalm.

> [1] The LORD is my shepherd; I shall not want.

> [2] He maketh me to lie down in green pastures:
> He leadeth me beside the still waters.

> [3] He restoreth my soul:
> He leadeth me in the paths of righteousness for
> His name's sake.

> [4] Yea, though I walk through the valley of the shadow
> of death, I will fear no evil: for thou art with me;
> thy rod and thy staff they comfort me.

> [5] Thou preparest a table before me in the presence of
> mine enemies: thou anointest my head with oil;
> my cup runneth over.

> [6] Surely goodness and mercy shall follow me all the
> days of my life: and I will dwell in the house of the
> LORD forever.

God had turned His back on me. I screamed out, "Thou *aren't* with me." No response. But, who could blame Him. I am evil, pure evil.

On that dark, cold night along the lakeshore, I had dreams and saw visions. I heard voices crying out from eternal agony. I smelt my syrupy guilt as it seeped from my pores to shroud my soul in shame. I saw my past. Every disgusting sin I had ever committed was revealed to me, in high definition clarity. I saw lies, anger, manipulation, gossip, pride, debauchery, sexual immorality, lust, drunkenness, and detestable idolatry.

Brother, I was in mortal pain. Disgust filled my sense. Mutilated from the inside out, the taste of secreted filth dripped from my lips. I had reached my final breaking point. All that saved me, for that moment, my rage exploded outward.

My visions turned to the world. Ugly, sad and disgusting were the images that revealed themselves to me. Poverty, war, disease, and deception of every kind. I saw evil in action; corporate lies, government cover-ups and hatred disguised in a cloak of religion self-righteousness. I could see no hope for this world.

Next, my most horrific encounters. The visions of those I had harmed on my walk through this life. I saw their tears, I heard their cries. I felt *their* pain. The agony I felt was their agony. The harm I had caused. The evils I had placed on them. I fell to the ground and cried.

God, why have you forsaken me? I offered you my life. You promised to never leave me. And this is what I get from you?

The skies howled and a cold, hard rain began to fall.

Drenched in sorrow, a nightmarish delirium dictated my next vision. I was surrounded by those who had sinned against me. I saw the faces of those who had made a conscious decision to take advantage, to destroy, or to hurt. I became enraged, *pissed*! I hated! Everyone and everything! Bastards, all of you. Selfish bastards, all so *fucking righteous*. Blameless, aren't you! You too, bitch! I don't need you. I don't need your shit. I only hope that someday *you* are forced to this place, this place of torment.

Just go to hell, all of you!

You too, *great almighty*!

The night turned still. Silence entombed my soulless spirit.

Through the murk, fueled by the force of my fury, I made my way back to Paradiso. Pleading with the gods to bring daylight, I must escape this agonizing dominion of darkness. The sun had yet to reach the mountain peaks that surround my valley of regret; my new dwelling place.

My garden of doom.

As the darkness cradled me, I found myself on my knees, doubled over, holding my stomach. My breath was taken from me. My heart heaved from my chest. Vomit, with the warmth of fresh blood, gushed from my mouth and nostrils. I was fading, dying on the shore of Lake Lugano.

Alone.

I stared out to the mist as it levitated from the warm waters of the lake. With my back to the darkness, facing east, I wept.

*God, why?*

I stomached my fate.

# chapter sixteen

Silvio was somewhat right about one thing. Now that I fully know evil, I *need* to know God. Yet, why would God want to know me given my evil ways? Hell, my sins of the past 48 hours were sufficient to secure eternal damnation.

Still on my knees, I looked up to the heavens. The rolling clouds traversed the sky revealing the morning stars. The last few drops of night's tears fell to earth. Above the mountains to my east, the colors of orange, violet and gold spilled out across the horizon. The early morning mist lofted from the lake, swirling about me like thousands of tiny white butterflies, besieging my spirit. As the winds picked up, the sound of leaves rustling in the breeze filled the air.

I imagined the breath of God.

*I am the Alpha and the Omega,*
*who is, and who was,*
*and who is to come,*
*the Almighty.*

My hallucinations flashed back from Luna's drugging, or whatever the hell that was. I hoped she had put something in my tea. If she hadn't, then the alterations within my mind would surely call for a diagnosis of acute psychoses.

I had lost touch with reality.

*I am the way and the truth and the life.*

Lost, hopeless and destined for God knows what, I drew ever closer to total madness. Fear encased my soul. The internal conflict that gripped me, ripped me into a million little pieces. Exhaustion stole the last morsel of my strength. This world had become too much for me to take.

*Come to me, you who are weary and burdened*
*and I will give you rest.*

The realization sliced through my brain with the precision of a coroner's hand conducting an autopsy. I was mad. Completely off my frickin' rocker. I needed help. And now I'm hearing *voices.* I've finally reached that level of insanity that will require I be institutionalized. Locked up! Far away from Silvio.

*You, my brothers, were called to be free.*
*But do not use your freedom to indulge the sinful nature;*
*rather, serve one another in love.*

The voices persisted. Irritated, I answered.

I've heard all your promises before God. But, where in the hell are you now? Where in this world filled with injustice are you now? Where in this world of pain are you hiding? If you were here, caring for this sinner's paradise, I wouldn't be in this place of spiritual blight. Don't blame me! I came to you for a *purpose.* Remember? Nice purpose, God.

I'm tired. Tired of your promises. Tired of your empty words of love and peace. Tired of your followers' judgments. Tired of *In God We Trust.* Now that's an outright lie!

Tears flooded my eyes.

I thought we were to be *One* in You. All different parts of the same *Body.* How's that workin' for ya' God? Where's the truth? Where's the love in this world You created? This world of deceit!

My rage against the heavens above only served to intensify my severance from God – my evil sinful nature.

The skies flashed brilliantly. Thunder rolled densely from the peaks of the mountains to the depths of my despair. Lightning reached down from the heavens and electrified the waters just off the shoreline from where I knelt. Sparks shot upward to fill the morning mist, a force so strong it awakened my spirit and stirred my soul.

In that momentary burst of illumination, everything became peculiarly real. Total silence fell upon my surroundings. All sensation was stolen from my body. I felt light, airy. Peaceful. My eyes were drawn toward the waters. I saw a heavenly spirit, dressed in pure white. Approaching, amid the mist, that specter of Light bestowed upon me holy words of inspired imminence.

*Well, now. You certainly are way in*
*over your head this time, my child.*

*How did you ever let evil carry you so far from me?*

185

I was in the presence of the Lord, God Almighty, in the *flesh*. Jesus! I had never even considered trying to fathom this moment, the moment I would meet my maker. My exhilaration grew with my every breath. That is, if I'm actually still alive. A matter I really wasn't quite sure of at the moment.

> *Do you not know? It is written:*
> *'Do not put the Lord your God to the test.'*

With Jesus standing over me, I struggled to make sense of what was happening. Am I facing my final judgment? Is this my personal doomsday? And what's this about testing God? Hey Jesus, I don't test the Lord. I love my God, I negotiated.

> *Away from me, Satan! For it is written:*
> *'Worship the Lord your God, and serve Him only.'*

Great, now I have Jesus calling me Satan. I'm in a heap of trouble. As I knelt down in awe, I began to strategize. How in the hell am I going to convince God I'm not some devil? – I knew there was no humanly possible way to pull that off.

Jesus sat down on the grass next to me. Peace fell upon my soul. I turned to the Lord and crossed my legs to rest next to Him.

I confessed my sins. I am so sorry Jesus, but I am evil. Ok, I'll be perfectly honest with you, it's worse than that. I believe I've made a deal I can't get out of, a deal with the devil. I have betrayed you Jesus. I am a Judas.

*I know your anguish. I feel your pain. I have faced the struggles of this world. Evil lives among you. Every sheep is lost. Each child suffers. I cry for you all. I lived and died for you. I came to bring you peace. So why have you repaid good with evil?*

I knew I had taken that bite of the forbidden fruit of Eden. I knew good and evil. Jesus was right, I took the good He gave me and turned it toward my own selfish desires. I admitted my guilt to the Lord.

*I am the vine, you are the branches. He who abides in me, and I in him, bears much fruit. And right now, you really aren't doing very well at bearing good fruits. You know I have chosen you and given you gifts to be shared with the world. Gifts that are for the good of my kingdom.*

Again, He was right. (Jesus, two and me, nothing.) I know I've really been struggling for some time now. But, what is it that you expect of me, Lord? I mean, I'm only human.

*My buddy Paul eloquently explained the basics in a letter to the early church in Rome.*

> *Love must be sincere. Hate what is evil; cling to what is good. Be devoted to one another in brotherly love. Honor one another above yourselves. Never be lacking in zeal, but keep your spiritual fervor, serving the Lord.*
>
> *Be joyful in hope, patient in affliction, faithful in prayer. Share with God's people who are in need.*

His words ripped my heart in two. I was loving evil, *knowing* evil. My pride fell low in the depths of my sorrow. I was ashamed.

Jesus continued.

> *Bless those who persecute you; bless and do not curse. Rejoice with those who rejoice; mourn with those who mourn. Live in harmony with one another. Do not be proud, but be willing to associate with people of low position. Do not be conceited.*
>
> *Do not be overcome by evil, but overcome evil with good.*

That's a heavy one, Jesus. You ask a lot.

*Yeah, I know.*

What He had to say made a lot of sense. *Love must be sincere. Hate what is evil and cling to what is good. Be devoted to one another in brotherly love.* It just isn't within my strength to be *that* perfect. And I don't see many of those qualities expressed by your church these days, I shared in my defense.

*Some things never seem to change. And you know, that really ticks me off. During my time on this earth, the Pharisees and teachers of the Law could not grasp the New Covenant – the law of love and forgiveness. I had hoped they would've figured it out by now. For God did not send his Son into the world to condemn the world, but to save the world through Him. It's sad to say, but the church keeps having difficulty with that one. My family is to love and care for one another, not judge one another.*

But Jesus, why are we doing such a lousy job with the simplest of things you ask of us? Love one another and do not judge. They are so basic in principle, but so damned difficult in practice. It just seems America has lost her soul somewhere along the way.

I felt my temperature rise as I again considered the injustices of our world. Here we are in the 21st century and the wealthiest of nations isn't providing basic healthcare for its people! Didn't Jesus tell us to care for those who are sick? I know the arguments. Sure, the poor can go to pretty much any hospital and receive care. Then they can't pay (let alone purchase prescriptions) because feeding their family is essential, not their ridiculously outrageous medical bills, which results in their credit getting trashed. In a corporate-based society where one's credit score is your ticket to the American Dream, we have stepped on the poor once again.

Nothin' like keeping the working class in their place!

Isn't that what we're doing? We're all like a bunch of arrogant bullies maintaining our dominance at the local playground. Our problem only worsens when those bullies grow up to lead corporations and governments. Decisions are based on the dollars, not the people. Hell, we may have avoided the messy Mexican immigration issues we face today, if only *yesterday* we'd truly loved our neighbor as our self. I would bet it's pretty damn difficult to live just south of wealth and not want to pursue the same dreams.

Jesus, I guess I've just reached a point of frustration with both politics and religion in my country. The separation of church and state is a farce. Freedom and faith have been replaced with arrogance and bigotry. The church is driving segregation based on denominational biases. So many congregations have made it their *mission* to control others through political power. The church has let us down! If we, as a body, spent our time, money and energy on providing for the *least of these,* rather than fighting social issues like gay marriage and politically regulated value systems, maybe we could usher in a new *Era of Love.* Letting love control us, not us fighting to control others. At the very least, can't we simply care for the health needs of ALL Americans? I mean, doesn't it seem like *that* should be a basic *human* right in the *greatest nation of them all!*

And Jesus, didn't you say *he who is without sin, throw the first stone?* I sure see a lot of stones being tossed around by your followers. Are we ever going to get it?

*Above all, love each other deeply, because love covers over a multitude of sins. Each of you should use whatever gift you have received to serve others, as faithful stewards of God's grace in its various forms.*

Sure, I've heard that all my life. Even from those who blindly do the exact opposite. Look to the pages of the Old Testament. They're filled with the lurid affairs and selfish desires of righteous men. Even Abraham tried to create his heir by sleeping with his servant! And he was your chosen one to be the *father of many nations.*

A good intention only offers empty hope.

Ok, this is important folks. Abraham, a.k.a. Abram, is central to the whole story of our world.

Then, and now!

So, to save you the time of doing a Wikipedia on it, I've paraphrased it for you here.

> His original name was Abram meaning either "exalted father" or "my father is exalted." For the latter part of his life, he was called Abraham, "father of many nations."

> Judaism, Christianity and Islam are sometimes referred to as the Abrahamic religions, because of the role Abraham plays in their holy books and beliefs.

> In the Jewish tradition, he is called "Abraham, our Father". God promised Abraham that through his offspring, all the nations of the world will come to be blessed (Genesis 12:3), interpreted in Christian tradition as a reference to Christ. Jews, Christians, and Muslims consider him father of the people of Israel through his son Isaac (Exodus 6:3, Exodus 32:13).

> For Muslims, he is a prophet of Islam and the ancestor of Muhammad through his other son Ishmael. By his concubine, Keturah (Genesis 25), Abraham is also a progenitor of the Semitic tribes of the Negev who trace

their descent from their common ancestor Sheba (Genesis 10:28).

Consistent with the kinship pattern revealed in Genesis 4 and 5, Abraham married one wife. Her name was Sarah.

I guess that makes Sarah the mother of many nations (and Keturah the mother of Islam).

Jesus responded.

*As it is written, for though a righteous man falls seven times, he rises again, but the wicked are brought down by calamity.*

His words reverberated in my head, familiar words. As I pondered his statement, I realized I'd heard a similar message from those twentysomethings of the elite in Bangladesh.

"Calamity will fall upon the infidels."

*You must understand, My Father's ways are not the ways of this world. Seek first my kingdom and my righteousness. If you sincerely and actively seek my ways, you will find in yourself the strength to love and forgive. Gain the knowledge of all things holy. Be humble. We are all connected. One in spirit. Love your brothers and sisters, despite the transgressions you feel they are making. Despite your differences. I first loved you, regardless of your sins. In me, you have forgiveness. And yes, there are responsibilities.*

*But, all things must first begin with love.*

His Word was written on my heart. Those starving children of India and Bangladesh are my personal responsibility. They're my brothers and sisters, my children, as are all the children of the world. I have always believed Jesus to be a social activist. One who is radical when it comes to the *status quo*. As He walked this earth, Jesus spoke out against the arrogant leadership of the day, with extreme vigilance. And He has made it eternally clear; we are to feed those who are hungry, care for those who are sick.

To love our neighbors as ourselves.

*And commune with me. Walk with me and talk with me! I am with you always. Feel my presence within your spirit. My Holy Spirit, living in you. I'm here for you. When you are alone, I am there. When you're out with friends, I'm there, too. Include me in the conversation. I like a good party. I love meeting new people. And remember, you don't have to be so frickin' formal with me. We're family, bro!*

I saw Jesus in a whole new light. He really seemed pretty cool. The kind of guy I would like to call *brother*.

*I called you when you were but a child. Your life's path has always held a purpose. Although you have stumbled along the way, you were never alone. However, now you are at a defining moment. You can choose to fulfill your calling, or follow your own path. You hold the verdict in your hand. What's it gonna be boy? Yes or no? If you choose a holy life and devote yourself to the Father, you will hold a high place in my kingdom. A place with great responsibility, your role in my plan.*

Of course, my decision was an easy one to make. I mean, Jesus was sitting there right next to me, asking me to serve Him. What else could I do? I had to follow the way of my Lord. Besides, I wanted to know what destiny He had awaiting me. Maybe I could become a great teacher of His Word. That would be such an honor.

Jesus laughed. And laughed some more... a lot more, actually.

Smiling, he said, *Not many of you should presume to be teachers, my brother, because you know that those who teach will be judged more strictly. You all stumble in many ways. If anyone is never at fault in what he says, he is a perfect man, able to keep his whole body in check. No, my son, you are far from that level of character. Though I love you, regardless. You my friend, you are to be a **messenger**.*

Very cool! Jesus loves me in spite of myself. He has a job for me to do. What a concept! I knew it; I was called to the service of my Lord! Workin' for God. A man with a mission – a *messenger!* JC's PR dude. I can do that.

I began to reflect on the great messengers of the past. I first thought of John the Baptist. What a holy man, living by faith and spreading the good news.

*And don't forget our brother Martin. He is one of my finest creations.*

Martin Luther King, Jr. was a great man. A messenger, a leader, and a peacemaker. A man who shared the love of Jesus through his peaceful revolution of equality and concern for one another. Sadly, his words were too soon silenced. But his message continues to impact our world. A message that will live throughout eternity.

Then it hit me. Hey Jesus, do all your messengers face the same fate? Death! You failed to mention the hazards of the job. And that's a pretty damn big hazard!

Jesus assured, *Hey, Oprah's still going strong! That's yet another one of my most beautiful works. Not bad, huh?*

Yeah, and there's Bono too. What an amazing servant to the least of these. Still, I bet there's a *first-rate* security team that's got their backs.

*Your message is simple. You are to go out into the world and share the simplicity of my love. So many have gone astray, seeking truth where there is no light, worshipping false idols and the images of mere men, living as if there is no purpose to their lives. We are at a critical point. This is an era of change. A time when those who seek my ways will obtain the knowledge I have always promised.*

*Never fail to remember. – The ways of man shall never reveal the Kingdom of God.*

*If you follow me, I will give you the strength you need to fulfill your calling. My message to this hurting world has never changed. It is the Greatest Commandment of all.*

> *Love the Lord your God with all your heart and with all your soul and with all your mind. This is the first and greatest commandment.*

> *And the second is like it: Love your neighbor as yourself.*

> *See how that works? We are one.*

We talked for what seemed like an eternity. Jesus revealed many wonders and He offered me wondrous gifts to be shared with this world. But most of all, He gave me the *knowledge* of His precious love – his way of *being.*

From His Word, I was graced with a commission to communicate the power of His love – His message. But my message was extreme in comparison to the church leaders of today. My message to share is of His New Revolution. His radical message, found in the *red letters* of His Word.

> *You have heard that it was said, 'Love your neighbor and hate your enemy.' But I tell you: Love your enemies and pray for those who persecute you.*

*Do not judge, or you too will be judged. For in the same way you judge others, you will be judged, and with the measure you use, it will be measured to you.*

*So in everything, do to others what you would have them do to you, for this sums up the Law and the Prophets.*

The *do un* way of life! I grasped His message with brilliant clarity. A message of love, forgiveness and being one in spirit with all who walk this earth. At that moment, I saw a vision of the new heaven and earth. The coming of His *New Revolution.* A revolution of unity and renewal, by truly becoming one in His Spirit.

*The knowledge of the secrets of the kingdom of God has been given to you, but to others I speak in parables, so that, 'though seeing, they may not see; though hearing, they may not understand.'*

Why? That makes absolutely no sense Jesus, I pondered. I guess if His message was spelled out for us, there would be no need for faith. And faith is the essence of His way.

Hearing by faith, I listened to His Word.

*Who is wise and understanding among you? Let him show it by his good life, by deeds done in the humility that comes from wisdom.*

*But if you harbor bitter envy and selfish ambition in your hearts, do not boast about it or deny the truth. Such "wisdom" does not come down from heaven but is earthly, unspiritual, of the devil.*

*For where you have envy and selfish ambition, there you find disorder and every evil practice.*

*But the wisdom that comes from heaven is first of all pure; then peace-loving, considerate, submissive, full of mercy and good fruit, impartial and sincere.*

*Peacemakers who sow in peace raise a harvest of righteousness. (James 3:13-18)*

*The way to the new heaven and earth are found in each one of us. Peacemakers of one mind, spirit, heart, and soul. Our unity will beckon the Father's Kingdom and His perfect will. Please be as one in me.*

*This may be your last chance.*

Again, I'd heard a similar message already this weekend. Not the love part, but the critical point we're facing in our world. So I had to ask Jesus about 12212012 and 11:11.

*Which of you will listen to this or pay close attention in time to come? Who handed Jacob over to become loot, and Israel to the plunderers? Was it not the LORD, against whom we have sinned? For they would not follow his ways; they did not obey his law. So he poured out on them his burning anger, **the violence of war**. It enveloped them in flames, yet they did not understand; it consumed them, but they did not take it to heart.*

*Still, about that day or hour no one knows, not even the angels in heaven, nor the Son, but only the Father. I tell you this, offer your body as a living sacrifice holy and pleasing to God – this is your spiritual act of worship.*

Sure, the pressure is on again. Being holy and pleasing to God is quite the tall order. No one is perfect, JC.

*I did not come to heal the healthy, but to care for the sick. My love is sufficient for all your needs. You must have faith. It is through faith, the heart is purified. I know you're not perfect. Do you really think I'm so dim? The issue of perfection only becomes a problem when you begin to believe you are perfect, or better than your neighbor.*

*Surrender to me; let me be your brother, your friend. I will bless your life with the glory of my love.*

*And today, America needs my love desperately!*

His words comforted my soul. Jesus gets it. We do need His unity and love in this world. What we've tried for so long is obviously not working out very well. It's time for real change! We need to follow the Spirit that lives within each one of us to change this world of hurt. Once we share the gifts and knowledge God has given us, we can unite in His perfect way.

*I ask you, will you take up your cross and follow me?*

I couldn't let Jesus down. I mean, he was right there before me, asking me to serve Him. I was in awe. My answer was direct. Yes, Lord. I will follow you. I am prepared to devote my life to you. I am prepared to love my neighbor. I will be your *messenger*.

Jesus hugged me and kissed me. I felt an extraordinary closeness, a bond with my Lord. A brotherhood.

Prince of Peace, now that we're one, there is a question I really need an answer to. It's a tough one to broach. But, it's one I've struggled with most of my life. Jesus, when smokin' weed, I experience such a deep sense of communion with you. Is that wrong?

*I get that one all the time,* Jesus said while smiling.

Somehow, He reminded me of that guy on the pack of papers. I smiled back at my Lord.

*All things are lawful, but not all things are beneficial. All things are lawful, but you shall not be mastered by anything.*

*Seek me and I will lead you in the ways of my love.*

*If you want rules, take a look at our Father's Top Ten List. That will give you a pretty good understanding of what is holy and wise. Yet, I have come in place of the law, offering your freedom. My love is sufficient for all your needs, and you'll like it much more than the alternative.*

*Remember – you know me.*

Jesus described the *"nothing is a miracle"* perspective quite clearly.

*Furthermore, since they did not think it worthwhile to retain the knowledge of God, he gave them over to a depraved mind, to do what ought not to be done. They have become filled with every kind of wickedness, evil, greed and depravity. They are full of envy, murder, strife, deceit and malice. They are gossips, slanderers, God-haters, insolent, arrogant and boastful;* **they invent ways of doing evil;** *they disobey their parents; they are senseless, faithless, heartless, ruthless. Although they know God's righteous decree that those who do such things deserve death, they not only continue to do these very things but also approve of those who practice them.*

*Beyond that, you'd need to check with William Randolph Hearst for the answer to America's position on the matter of marijuana.*

I knew what he was talking about. Hearst and his "reefer madness" style propaganda campaign, which led to the 1937 criminalization of marijuana. Corporate driven laws, which limit personal freedoms while promoting the abuse of our constitution. It was all about hemp, a cheaper renewable resource, that if again legalized would positively impact our carbon footprint by reducing the use of fossil fuels and trees in numerous manufacturing processes. And hemp is a non-mood enhancer. Its cousin cannabis holds that gift.

Then there's the whole medical marijuana scam. That's just another example of putting the ideals of a few ahead of the needs of others. Besides, the stuff grows like a weed! Think how much money the pharmaceuticals would lose if patients could harvest their own treatment.

Most importantly, nobody beats their spouse or kids while smokin' pot. That's reserved for the *legal* demon in the bottle. From my experience, people become more expressive and loving toward one another, in a family kind of way. Smoke has a way of establishing a unique bond among perfect strangers who connect with other like minds. I've experienced the overwhelming power of Jesus' love while sharing life with a new friend, enjoying that gift of nature, God's creation.

And, it is written, *On the third day God said, "Let the land produce vegetation seed-bearing plants and trees on the land that bear fruit with seed in it, according to their various kinds."*

*And it was so. The land produced vegetation: plants bearing seed according to their kinds and trees bearing fruit with seed in it according to their kinds.*

*And God saw that it was good. And there was evening, and there was morning. (Genesis 1:11-13)*

Very cool, that Jesus. Sounds like He's a night person, too. What a God! He's my Savior. Still, I wasn't sure if He ever really answered my question. Just more parables. – Man, that Jesus sure makes you think.

*My message is about freedom and truth, not rules or oppression. Read my Word! A sin is a sin, and no one is perfect.*

My Bible had miraculously found its way from my bag to rest in the palm of my hand. It opened. Flipping through the pages of that little red book I randomly stopped on 1 Timothy, Chapter 4 – instructions to Timothy, a young believer, from his friend the Apostle Paul. I read the words aloud.

> [1]The Spirit clearly says that in later times some will abandon the faith and follow deceiving spirits and things taught by demons. [2]Such teachings come through hypocritical liars, whose consciences have been seared as with a hot iron. [3]They forbid people to marry and order them to abstain from certain foods, which God created to be received with thanksgiving by those who believe and who know the truth. [4]For everything God created is good, and nothing is to be rejected if it is received with thanksgiving, [5]because it is consecrated by the word of God and prayer.

> [6]If you point these things out to the brothers, you will be a good minister of Christ Jesus, brought up in the truths of the faith and of the good teaching that you have followed. [7]Have nothing to do with godless myths and old wives' tales; rather, train yourself to be godly. [8]For physical training is of some value, but godliness has value for all things, holding promise for both the present life and the life to come.

> [9]This is a trustworthy saying that deserves full acceptance [10](and for this we labor and strive), that we have put our hope in the living God, who is the Savior of all men, and especially of those who believe.

> [11]Command and teach these things. [12]Don't let anyone look down on you because you are young, but set an example for the believers in speech, in life, in love, in faith and in purity. [13]Until I come, devote yourself to the public reading of Scripture, to preaching and to teaching.

<sup>14</sup>Do not neglect your gift, which was given you through a prophetic message when the body of elders laid their hands on you.

<sup>15</sup>Be diligent in these matters; give yourself wholly to them, so that everyone may see your progress. <sup>16</sup>Watch your life and doctrine closely. Persevere in them, because if you do, you will save both yourself and your hearers.

Jesus asked, without speaking, if I understood His Word, *this time.* Yes, for the first time, I listened. His precepts became clear – obvious. His is a doctrine of hope. Hope in the living God, who is the Savior of all men, and especially of those who believe.

Remember Judgment Day, you animal!

What's so wrong with being a living example for others in speech, in life, in love, in faith and in purity? Those aren't rules; they're the natural desires of our spirit. And, a beautiful perspective from which to view the grandeur of our world.

The knowledge and depth of insight Jesus imparted ignited my spirit. A passion for His ways flowed within, embracing my soul. Peace and hope fell upon me.

*One thing you lack. Go, sell everything you have and give to the poor, and you will have treasure in heaven. Then come, follow me.*

I couldn't tell if He was being serious or not. He couldn't be. Give up all my stuff, and then follow Him? Hey, I know lots of wealthy Christians. Why am I being singled out? That's not fair!

*Believe me. I've cut you a lot of slack, bro. Take me at my word. If you love me, you will keep my commands. Go out and share my message.*

*This is the time of kingdoms falling.*

At this point, Jesus took my hand and asked me to pray with Him. From His touch, I felt the eternal power of my God.

> *Our Father in heaven, hallowed be your name,* ***your kingdom come, your will be done on earth as it is in heaven.*** *Give us this day our daily bread.* ***Forgive us our trespasses, as we forgive those who trespass against us.*** *And lead us not into temptation, but deliver us from the evil one.*

Amen!

*For if you forgive men when they sin against you, your heavenly Father will also forgive you. But if you do not forgive men their sins, your Father will not forgive your sins.*

Damn, that Jesus sure expects a lot.

Jesus continued, *for it is written,*

*You were dead in your transgressions and sins, in which you used to live when you followed the ways of this world and of the ruler of the kingdom of the air, the spirit who is now at work in those who are disobedient.*

*All of us also lived among them at one time, gratifying the cravings of our sinful nature and following its desires and thoughts. Like the rest, we were by nature objects of wrath.*

*Because of his great love for us, God, who is rich in mercy, made us alive with Christ. For it is by grace you have been saved, through faith—and this not from yourselves, it is the gift of God— not by works, so that no one can boast. For we are God's workmanship, created in Christ Jesus to do good works, which God prepared in advance for us to do.*

*Go out into the world and share my love. Love to the measure our Father has blessed you. Seek knowledge. And share the knowledge that I have offered all of you. Join with one another to beckon our New Revolution.*

*Oh, and one more thing.*

*I AM the Universe, but - the name is Jesus!*

Jesus and I embraced. He then turned to move beyond. My Lord offered a wave to reassure me with His love – *a real, everlasting love*. He faded from sight.

*Know that I am with you always, to the very end of the age.*

# chapter seventeen

I awoke hot and sweaty from the early morning sun beating down on my body. The winds of last night's storm had calmed. I had not. The flowering gardens of Eden, which hid me from the promenade's morning guests, still hung low with millions of water droplets. Light passing through each liquid crystal cast off the hues of life, glistening around me like a kaleidoscope of illusion. My eyes attempted to focus. I arched my back in an effort to ease the pain acquired from passing out on the hard, cold earth. Had I only made it a few blocks further, I could have peacefully passed out in my semi-comfortable Holiday Inn bed.

Ok, what in the *holy hell* just happened? I reached for my phone to check the hour as I staggered toward a long, hot shower, avoiding eye contact with my fellow trekkers along the streets of Paradiso. A somehow familiar walk of shame. And coffee, I need a *strong* Italian coffee. And smokes. Damn, I need a cigarette. And maybe a shot. Or five! What in the hell's happening to me in this den of iniquity? I don't *even* want to think about it. Thank God that's easy for me to do in the morning – not think. *God?* While still maintaining a sleepy self-control, I feared an impending panic attack. But, I just don't panic!

It was 08:57, according to my Nokia. I gathered my bearings as I headed to the hotel. Last night was clearly going to take some serious mental acrobatics to decipher. What the hell did Luna slip me? *Dude*, what a night! I thought I talked to God! Hell, I thought I had sex with Satan!

So damn real! Shivers ran cold through my veins. It was all so damn *surreal*.

Finally a friendly face, I thought as I pushed open the door of the hotel bar revealing the ever-present Angelo.

"*Buon giorno*, my American friend. Happy Monday! How are you enjoying this glorious morning in paradise?"

He had no idea. I mustered a smile and greeted him with an uncertain nod.

Upon a second take, Angelo followed, "Well, look. What did the cat drag in?"

Close enough for a foreigner, I smiled.

"Perhaps we are just now arriving home from our encounter with last night's tantalizing mirage."

Angelo gave me a guilty smirk. The kind your mom gave you when rolling in all red-eyed and smelling of cigarette smoke, well after curfew.

"What else can I get you?" he said while preparing my morning drug.

I needed smokes.

"Of course. Water and an OJ, too?"

I said no to the OJ, as it reminded me of another really evil spirit. Besides, there was already enough acid in my stomach. Angelo tossed me a box of Marlboro Lights. I packed them in the palm of my hand, until realizing that thumping sound was echoing way too loudly in the empty chamber sitting atop my neck. I had one match left. I lit a smoke.

Placing that cup of steaming adrenalin in front of me, Angelo observed, "You appear out of sorts this morning. Too much fun last night? Or, are you dreading your departure from Lugano?"

My dread came from being *in* Lugano. At this point, the chaos of India or Bangladesh would offer more peace than this place. I told Angelo I would be staying on for awhile longer. Not at the hotel, but here in Lugano. And I've gotta get a move on. I have an important meeting at 11:00, sharp.

"You were warned! Three days is not nearly enough time to be consumed by this paradise. In your case, it appears she won't even let you out of her clutches. Or, was it last night's adventure that has you in the grasps of this worldly delight?"

Last night's adventure was right. Not necessarily Luna, but all that she represented. My guilt consumed me. I was worn, I shared with Angelo. There were things that had happened during my visit to Paradiso. Things that I could not explain. Frightening things.

"My brother, I am here just for you. Tell me what you have seen. I will offer you guidance. Trust me to direct you. That's why I am here. But, you must first ask."

Brothers of the dark side, I feared. I sucked down my glass of water in one continuous gulp. The caffeine didn't seem to make a dent in my conscious mind. I needed a hot shower. Karim would be arriving soon, but the coffee was still too hot for me to slam and run. I grabbed another smoke. I need a light, I mumbled to Angelo while my next Marlboro hung from my mouth.

"You're in luck. These arrived just this morning," he said while tearing open a package wrapped in plain white paper to retrieve a box of matches. "Special delivery, for our special guest. You Daniel."

From the far end of the counter, Angelo tossed that little brown box full of fire directly toward my place at his bar. As it drifted through the air, twirling, as if in slow motion, I determined it best not to attempt a catch. I would have just looked foolish scrambling for something out of thin air at this hour of the day.

With the anticipation of my next morning smoke, I watched that box land directly on the bar in front of me, spinning and sliding into place. Squarely located just within my reach sat that little brown box with gold lettering. Just one word was printed across its background.

That word drove a spike deep into my heart.

Just one word.

*Lucifers.*

His words forced their way upon my soul with a chilling resemblance to our sexual encounter of last night.

*"I will be in touch with you first thing Monday morning. I must know all about your weekend."*

Silvio, you evil bastard!

"What is it my brother? I can see the rage in your eyes."

That's it. I quit! These things are evil! I cried out while throwing that nearly full pack of smokes back at Angelo. Maybe some other distressed traveler could use them. But not me, I've smoked my last. – I quit!

"What? – Why the change of heart?"

Control! Those cowboy weeds had a hold on me. I'm tired of allowing evil to stand in my way. I was sickened by the evils in my heart, the filth of my world. I needed a shower, and now. I told Angelo I would stop in to say farewell once I finished getting ready and had checked out. Hopefully by then, I'd be a little more coherent and possibly hold a single thought.

Time was short. Karim was coming soon. I headed for the door while still studying that box of matches grasped in my hand. As I neared the exit, Angelo got all intense on me.

"Brother, remember you are never alone on this journey. You have a power within your soul that can carry you through the darkest of days. You hold that secret within your heart. Never let your faith in the truth fade. You hold the key to eternity within your spirit. Use that gift. Filter each decision you face in this life through the beauty of that gift. *Become one with the spirit within you.*"

❧❧

I know lucifers are just another name for matches. Still, I couldn't ignore the paradoxical nature of all the happenings dancing around me. The good and evil of my world, which I had for so long maintained in a delicate balance, was now tilting out of control.

Trepidation filled my soul as the fog lifted from my head. It was like coming out of a dream in reverse. The more I focused on that nightmare, the clearer my recollections became. Yet, my logic was hidden in a house of mirrors; too many reflections to make anything out as truth.

I just wish I had my *fucking* passport!

The shower was helpful in drawing me out of the haze. With my room looking as if it had not been used, I did a last minute check to see that I'd gathered all my stuff. When one is traveling light, only the essentials are carried. And I am not about to lose any of my essentials. I like my stuff.

The door slammed behind me and I was off to the tiny metal chamber they call an elevator. Just enough time to pay my debts and say goodbye to Angelo. There was something peaceful about that fellow, I considered while abruptly dropping six floors to land in the lobby.

One would think, during Monday morning checkout, my wonderful hosts at Holiday Inn Hell would have someone other than their senile grandma to man the front desk. Slow was an understatement, and of course – *no Inglese.*

Karim pulled up in his shimmering Benz, still damp from an apparent recent washing, as I was attempting to communicate my room number and name to Grandma. He jumped out of the car with a smile and waved through the plate glass window. He seemed happy, excited. I figured Karim enjoys a roadtrip as much as I do. He was obviously stoked for his journey to Spain. Nearly bouncing off the walls, he entered the Holiday Inn with a boisterous greeting.

"My brother, good morning. Today is a glorious day!" Reaching forward with a hug he said, "I'll take your bags to the car."

I smiled back and asked if he could give me a hand with Grandma. I needed a translator. I was beginning to worry that she'd keel over at any moment. Karim assisted in the check-out transaction, and the niceties. Grandma and I smiled at one another. She really did seem sweet. I was just in a rush.

Karim grabbed my bags. I told him I'd be right out. I had to say goodbye to the bartender. Actually, there was something I needed to ask Angelo. He was appearing more like one of the good guys, not a brother in my evil little Society. His words offered an extraordinary comfort to me this morning. But, something he had said earlier left me questioning my options in this life. I almost felt a glimmer of hope when I reflected on his statement.

Having completed my transaction with that smiling gray-haired mom-figure, I turned and walked to the door of Angelo's establishment. Grandma spoke out in a garbled array of words. I turned and waved goodbye. Friendly old broad, I thought.

The door fell heavy to my touch as I attempted my grand entrance. I pushed harder. It didn't budge. Opening this door was never so difficult before, I pondered.

"*Rinnovo*," Grandma cried out.

I turned yet again and wished her *rinnovo*, as well. I was really getting the hang of this language. It even sounds *Italiana* when I speak their words.

I gave the door a manly jab, to no avail. I figured it must be locked. I tried to ask Grandma where Angelo went off to. He knew what time I was leaving, I grimaced.

"*Angelo*? No Angelo."

Karim gave the horn a blast. Apparently he didn't want me to be late for my meeting, and he's probably anxious to hit the road. I'm sure he's primed for the adventure awaiting him. I scribbled Angelo's name on the back of my business card and handed it to Grandma to pass along.

"Angelo?"

I confirmed with a thumbs up. She just stood there holding the card.

*Rinnovo*, I saluted as my final farewell.

With a swoosh of the automatic sliding door of Holiday Inn Lugano, I left my weekend retreat in Paradiso behind. It was a glorious day. The sun was bright. The air was cool. A soft breeze lifted the palm branches, gently waving so long. Nature's perfect fanfare. However, I wasn't feeling victorious at the moment.

The reality of my predicament was finally settling in. It was Monday morning and my time had come to face the music. I had to meet with my uncle. He held my passport, he held my future. I had made a commitment. I knew there was no escaping my fate; no evading the reaches of the Brotherhood of the Passage. I knew too much. I knew the secrets of our Society, and our universe. I knew the *number* – 12212012.

There was simply no escaping my destiny.

For a brief second, I debated on telling Karim to go on without me. Maybe I should call and tell my brothers I'd changed my mind. Maybe, they would accept my apology and return my passport. Maybe, I could gain their forgiveness and go on with my life.

That was my desire.

One thing I did know. I wanted something more out of life.

A change.

But, I also knew something else.

I can't change.

# chapter eighteen

Karim was obviously ready to get a move on. I jumped in the backseat to settle in for the short ride to Banque UniSuisse. Not only had Karim detailed the exterior of his Mercedes for the big trip, but the interior was sparkling as well. Anticipation impregnated the atmosphere within the shell of Karim's luxurious world. Even the carpet was standing at attention, freshly vacuumed and doused with air freshener for his big excursion.

That aroma took me back to Dubai. It had a definite Middle Eastern essence. Sweet, yet with an herbal bite. One that was common in taxis throughout that part of the world. Dubai was truly amazing. The unimaginable wealth in that city made me drunk with envy. Oh, and those beautiful Middle Eastern woman. They do know how to treat a man. And their *eyes*. It could all be mine, I deliberated.

Hell, it's already mine! I've got a deal. I'm *the man.*

I began to reconsider my position, sinking deep into the folds of my leather seat. The thought of the money, the lifestyle, lured me into a deep trance. My destiny was upon me. Excitement drew the calm from every layer of my being. I was nervous about the decision I made, the decision forced upon me by the Universe.

I thought of Jesus.

I was perplexed.

My reasoning mind quickly returned to deliberate.

I am *the man*! My defensiveness grew fierce with the force of the *spirit of the air.* Living in The Mansion; now that's a *hell-of-a-lot* better than giving up everything and following some illusion offered me by last night's hallucinogen. And if you think about it, I have nothin' to worry about. I already have that base covered. I was *saved* as a child. Once saved, always saved!

Right? I questioned. I felt my spirit stumble.

I'll have to find one of the denominations that uphold that doctrine. If they're wrong, at least it won't be my fault. – Damn, I really am just like those religious jerks. Find the coalition that suits your needs and biases. A mental image of Judas invaded my mind.

Sure, I immediately repressed that thought.

"So brother, what's your plan?" Karim looked me squarely in the eyes via his rearview mirror.

I showed him the same respect as I replied. I've made up my mind. It looks like Lugano is going to be my home for awhile. There certainly are worse places to set up camp. I know. I've experienced them recently. My meeting this morning is really just a formality. The deal has already been consummated, I explained. Today is simply to finalize the details.

"Ah yes, and the devil is in the details," Karim said smiling broadly.

I've never been one to concern myself with the details. The big picture is where I put my trust. As for the devil, let's hope not.

Enough about me. I changed the subject. I really was curious about Karim's upcoming journey.

"Here," he said while offering a map of Europe. "I have it all plotted out. My final destination is Vigo, Spain. Vigo is one of the country's larger metropolitan areas. It's a city with a style, a vibe, a nightlife. But most impressive are Vigo's beautiful *muchachas*. And being on the west coast, the sunsets are to die for."

Vigo wasn't a city I'd ever heard of. I haven't really spent that much time in Spain. But, it's on my list.

"If you look at the map, you'll find my route."

Examining his Michelin Guide, striped in yellow highlighter, I followed the marked path with my finger. His trip was certainly not a direct route. Not that there really is one. I mentioned it appeared he had stops to make along the way.

"Yes, I have many contacts to meet, but the schedule is tight. My first stop is Torino. From there, an easy border crossing into France, and on to Monaco. I'll need a couple days in that beautiful asylum of wealth. Next is a quick detour to a delightful village in the hillsides of *Provence*, followed by the dreaded drive to Madrid. That's one long road trip. However, Vigo is the *finale*."

As I studied the map, I recalled the places I had visited along his charted path. I located Monaco and thought of that beautiful retreat a few kilometers away, *Villefranche-sur-Mer*. That seaside village where I first met Monique. I was sure to see her again, now that The Mansion is my home. I hoped she would forgive me. Reflecting on that night by the pool, I realized I must have been mad. What a beauty. What was I thinking?

My fantasy of Monique was abruptly interrupted by the whirling siren of a police car speeding past us. I glanced up at the rearview mirror to see if it made Karim sweat. My curiosity was getting the best of me. Not that I really thought that Karim was a terrorist or something, but he wasn't very forthcoming with the purpose of his journey. So, I just came right out and said it. W*hat're you up to, bro?* My lack of tact even surprised me. I corrected myself with a general query as to the purpose for his appointments.

"Oh, brother. If only we had the time I would tell you all about it. In brief, I can tell you that it's not a pleasure trip. Still, I assure you, I always find fun while on the way."

We both laughed; kindred spirits of the road, and preferably the back way. I always enjoy travel with a purpose. That is, so long as it doesn't get in the way of my fun. His upcoming adventure left me with a touch of jealousy.

The tires of Karim's Mercedes rumbled along the cobblestone streets of Lugano's business district as we approached the Banque UniSuisse headquarters. It was an impressive structure, looking all bank-like. Built of marble, brushed metal and glass, it stood out among its historic surroundings like a Matisse hanging in the Sistine Chapel. It looked great, but just a little out of place.

Karim pulled his taxi into a clearly marked area designated for loading and unloading of passengers only. The Swiss make their rules easily understood, in an unobtrusive sort of way. Just don't break one. They're likely to let you know about it. Switzerland – the nicest little police state one could ever visit. I gathered my backpack and checked for my phone.

Swinging open the door, Karim announced in his best official tone, "We have reached your destination, my fine sir."

I slowly moved out to the pavement. My lack of sleep and general lingering intoxication made me feel faint. I stood there, peering to the upper floor of the bank while Karim delivered my bags to my side. I must have appeared a penitent man gazing toward that temple to the God of Money, positioned directly across the traffic infested *strada*.

Karim questioned, "You haven't changed your destination yet again, have you?"

No, I assured him. This is something that I have to do. I am a man of my word. Beside, who knows what delights await me beyond the confines of my old life. I was prepared for my new assignment in this life. The measure of a man can be found in his commitment to his own words. I'm a man of action. I act on my promises.

I stood proudly on that street corner upon hearing my words of personal praise. I am an accomplished man, a charming man. No wonder they offered me such a high position within the Brotherhood. If I'd just been hired on as CEO of Microsoft I'd be dancing in the streets. I needed to capture that same level of enthusiasm for my new role of leadership within the Society, I convinced myself.

I turned toward Karim to say my final goodbyes. Directly behind him, two familiar faces quickly approached, Sa'eed and Colsante.

"Daniel! So good to see you my brother," Sa'eed announced.

"Today is the day of your appointment," Colsante added with an awkward pump of his fist.

As I debated on introducing my brothers to the taxi driver, Karim had already initiated a conversation with Sa'eed – in Arabic. Colsante and I looked at one another feeling at an obvious disadvantage.

Colsante rolled his eyes. "I really need to learn that language. Better to learn it now. Who knows, it may one day be the globally sanctioned tongue."

Finishing their brief conversation, Sa'eed turned to me. "Are you ready? You know Uncle Nuncio doesn't like to wait."

I told them to go ahead without me. I'd be right there. I needed to pay my driver and take a minute to prepare for this momentous occasion.

Once again, I turned to Karim for our parting words. I thanked my friend and wished him a *bon voyage*. I tipped over the top. Pretty much all I had in cash. From here on out, money will never be a consideration I must entertain.

"I'm sorry to see you go, my brother," Karim said with a sincere sadness in his eyes. "I've quickly established a connection with you. Don't ask me why. I just want good things to come your way. We face so many complexities in this world. I fight those demons daily. Demons that are poised to dramatically impact our future. I found you to be one that helped bring transparency to my obscurities. You have a gift. Thank you for sharing it with me."

I was truly touched. A plank lodged squarely in the back of my mouth. Fighting off a tear, I reached and embraced my brother. Karim's one of the good guys. I just knew it.

As I approached the crosswalk, Karim sped off with a blast of his horn and a wave out his window. Off to Vigo. I said a little prayer for him. I'm really going to miss that guy, I contemplated.

Sweat flushed my brow. It then rushed my entire body as the light turned to the international symbol for walk. I stepped into the crosswalk with my bags hanging heavy upon me. The rush of people on either side of me made my environment spin. I said a big prayer, for me.

The church bells echoed throughout Lugano, beginning their scheduled count of the hour, with rigid precision. This is Switzerland, you know. It was 11:00 in the morning. Not one of my favorite hours of the day. Succumbing to another flashback from Luna's poison, my body unexpectedly grew weaker. Dripping with perspiration, I questioned if I'd ever make it to the other side.

The second clang of the hour resounded ruthlessly in my head. My world turned psychedelic, fearful. Life began moving in stereo. Brilliant lights attached themselves to my pupils. The world around me became a twisted dreamscape. I was reeling. But I wasn't about to play up my breakdown. I'm a fighter.

The third toll of the hour welcomed me to the other side. Life became multi-dimensional. The sounds of the city passed through my brain with the hollowness of an AM Radio. The heightened intensity of my senses permitted me to hear each passerby's words with deafening exactness, simultaneously.

Through annoying static, I heard the words shared between lovers as they smiled into each other eyes. I heard the voices of children excited about the wonders of a new day. I heard the concerned words expressed by a young businessman as he assisted an elderly gentleman with his heavy load. I heard the appreciation expressed from within the old man's heart.

As the fourth toll rang out, it pierced my eardrums with the painfulness of fingernails scraping across a chalkboard. I nearly dropped to my knees. I stopped to catch my breath. Lucidity began to overtake me. My mind flashed out data and emotion from the events of last night, shown in the brilliance of Technicolor. My struggle for inner-peace erupted into a nuclear meltdown. Silvio's words intruded my heart.

*Live life on the edge,*
*believing that you are to take*
*whatever is placed before you.*
*Your gifts from the powers that be.*

*Life is about each of us reaching*
*our full potential – our destiny.*

*Self-actualization is that place*
*where we actually become like God.*
*To reach that level, you must learn to view*
*the world through your passions – that*
*which drives you from the heart.*

Those words reminded me of my fortune. My commitment to the Brotherhood. The desires of my heart. Saliva flooded my mouth. I went for a cigarette. They weren't there, just that damn box of matches. *Shit!* – I don't smoke.

The next toll sliced through my spirit to the depths of my soul. I felt His spirit alive in me. I fought it. The presence of Jesus and the depth of his Word enraged me. I don't want to think about God. I don't need the guilt trip, ok! I fiercely blocked the impulse to run.

Focusing outwardly at the toll of the sixth bell, the motion around me cut to a blur. In the flash of a freeze-frame, I saw her. Frozen in front of me, while the rest of the world passed her by. I remembered those freckles. The plumes of beautiful red hair.

Those pure blue eyes. That little turned up nose. But it was her habit that gave her away; that adorable little nun from the train station in Italy. She looked me in the eyes. Softly smiling, she waved. As that angel blended into the background of movement and light, I felt loved.

At the seventh clap of the hour, my awareness moved to another. A mother, with daughter in tow. As I looked upon that tiny smile, the eyes of a child reach into my soul. *Cindy Lou Who*, the little angel who welcomed me to Lugano, had crossed my path once again. I became emotional. A tear of joy ran down my face. I raised my hand to greet her. She knew me. She returned my greeting with a precious smile. I felt innocence.

The eighth toll brought clarity of mind. The motion around me slowed to a comfortable pace. I was regaining my sanity. My reality is simple. I *know* both good and evil.

I stepped toward the entry of Banque UniSuisse at the cry of the ninth chime. I was prepared to take my destiny like a man. I stood tall with confidence as I reached forward to buzz in the building. God only knows why, but at that moment I recalled the morning's words of wisdom shared from Angelo's lips.

*Become one with the spirit within you.*

I stopped dead in my tracks.

Upon the tenth slap of the clappers, Angelo called out to me.

"My brother, please wait!"

What in the hell's he doin' here? I stepped aside to allow those lined up behind me to enter the temple, secured by double locking doors to protect its treasures for evil thieves.

"I'm so happy I caught you. I was afraid I'd be too late. I know we didn't get a chance to say goodbye, but that's not why I came. I'm here for you; don't you see? Can't you trust the spirit within? I'm crossing a line here, and I could get into really big trouble over this one, but dammit Kev, for a smart guy, sometimes you are so *dense*! Open your soul. I beg you, please brother. Take another look inside. This is the time to heed the call!"

He continued with an urgent plea, "Please God! Send your love. Before it's too late!"

The final bell of the hour drew me back to the here and now.

"Brother, I'm so glad I caught you," Karim shouted from behind me, as he reappeared on the scene.

Totally caught off guard, I turned to make the introduction, but Angelo had vanished. As if into thin air, like a spirit.

"And who in the hell are you talking to, bro? You're lookin' a little crazy right now."

The illusions of my mind were maddening.

Karim apologized, "I hope I'm not overstepping my boundaries, but brother, I have concerns. It was something that your partner Sa'eed told me. It just didn't add up. Daniel, plain and simple, I don't trust that man."

I was late for my meeting. It was now past 11:00 and Uncle Nuncio was going to be royally pissed. And my passport – it's crucial I get it back. However, I know me. Once in the midst of such great powers, I will succumb to the desires of my heart. Still, Karim was right. My intuition told me the same thing. Down deep, I knew it all along. I didn't trust Sa'eed either.

I stood there at a crossroads, my defining moment. My brain was devoured by confusion. Nothing was making sense. I drew upon Angelo's words in an attempt to strangle the snake that had for so long lived within my bowels. Still, I questioned. Could I trust the Spirit? Could I abandon my old way of being and truly become *one* with the spirit within me?

It was at that moment of truth that I finally broke down and allowed my thoughts and feelings to be fully given over to the truth, the spirit within my soul. I *surrendered* to the power of love. I became one in spirit. It was at that moment that I broke my deal with the devil. The knowledge of God's love filled my heart. That holy encounter in the garden, just a few hours earlier, became vibrant. *Truthful*. The wisdom of His absolute truth was made real in me.

So, too, was the fact that evil lives.

Standing at the entrance of that shrine to the god of this world, I turned from evil and committed to act only in love. It was at that moment my divine destiny was fully revealed. Something that had been written on my heart for all eternity. – I was created to be a prophet, a *messenger* for my Lord.

A messenger of His Love.

"I have. I've overstepped my boundaries. I apologize. I'll be on my way," Karim said while offering another hug.

As we embraced, I realized that this man was a real friend. I could see it in his eyes. I felt it in my heart. I finally broke my silence, smiling into Karim's eyes.

Brother, who needs a frickin' passport, anyway? There's no adventure in that! Karim grinned, as if he knew something I didn't. I asked if he'd care to give a fellow fugitive a ride the hell out of this place.

Without a word, but with a wink and a smile on his face, Karim grabbed my bags and headed toward his illegally parked Mercedes. I followed, turning to look up at the top floor of the Banque UniSuisse building. I could see nothing from this angle, which means they probably couldn't see me either. I was walking away from the Brotherhood, the money, the lifestyle. I was giving up all that I own and all that I selfishly desired to follow the ways of Jesus.

Peace fell upon my soul.

"Here, quickly! No, the front seat. This is a free ride, my brother."

As I jumped in the car, Karim gunned it. I looked back toward my past destiny one last time. As we sped away, I saw four men running from that temple in all their fury. Heads turned to observe the commotion, as those four were scrambling, shouting and pointing, while desperately looking – for me. Each face I knew, one intimately.

Uncle Nuncio, Sa'eed, Colsante, and of course, Silvio.

Just beyond that foursome of evil stood an old woman, looking onward. Her head wrapped in a ragged brown shawl, smokin' a butt. My attention was drawn to her as I recognized that old lady from *Piazza della Riforma*. Peering out the rear window of our getaway car, she saw me. That blessed angel smiled and waved farewell.

It was a big smile.

I had escaped, for now. I knew evil would search the corners of the universe to find me, to make me pay the price for my verdict. But, I was ok with that. I had no fear. I just don't panic.

From within I heard His challenge.

*Through love, grow in knowledge and depth of insight.*

That's a required skill for a messenger, you know. I said a prayer
for my ex-brothers of the dark side.

Not a word was spoken until we were well away from Eden.
Karim looked as beleaguered as I was feeling. We were
ancestrally united; brother sharing true empathy. So much had
happened these past few days. I needed time to make sense of it
all. And time was something I had plenty of.

Breaking the silence, I asked Karim for the map. I looked to our
final destination, Vigo. I hadn't realized it's just over the border
from Portugal. I again recalled that little angel I met somewhere
along the way. Her name was Gazi. She told me about this fishing
and farming village just north of Porto. Her hometown, Lavra. I'll
have to look her up once we reach the end of the road. I mused.

Traveling the Roman roads, taking the way around, we fantasized
about our imminent adventure. It was sure to be a blast. Laughing,
we agreed the two of us made rather strange travel partners. An
Iraqi Muslim and an American Christian, although neither of us
had the papers to prove it.

Crossing over the border into Italy, I felt a sense of relief. I had
escaped the rule of Switzerland, and the Brotherhood of the
Passage. Sitting there in total silence, we both maintained pleasant
smiles. I believed Karim was happy to have me along for the ride.
I sure as hell was glad to have a friend like him, and thankful, too.
If it weren't for Karim's concern for a brother, I may never have
escaped the evils of Eden.

Speeding off to *Karim and Kev's Awesome European Adventure*,
I turned on his WorldSpace Satellite Radio. A favorite song from
my early years was just beginning to play. It was an old Todd

Rundgren tune, *Just One Victory*. As I listened to the words of that song, I wondered. Could it be that he's a *messenger* too?

Maybe there's a lot of us *unlikely messengers* out there.

As I ventured toward my new life, I admitted to myself – I made the right decision.

One that I could live with and one I could die with.

As their Mercedes Benz S-Class barreled down a remote back road in the Italian countryside, Karim and Kevin began to reflect on the countless coincidences that led them to this place in time. Amazed by the events that collided to create their newfound friendship, they felt united. Like real half-brothers. They laughed about the good times that surely awaited them on their way. And they laughed in the face of the demons that awaited them in battle.

But little did they know...

This was no coincidence.

This was their destiny.

Oh, and that *empty* Kipling backpack, obscured from sight, tucked away under the passenger seat of Karim's Mercedes.

They didn't know about that either.

# epilogue

That's where my personal *Jihad* [my *Revolution*] began. Since that fateful weekend, I've been running from the devil. The fervent dragnet of the *Brotherhood of the Passage* hasn't let up either. Evil finds me wherever I go. Thankfully the power of the *One* provides me with the strength I need to avert evil's wicked touch, at least most of the time.

Still, I must keep moving on.

The incessant tribulations I faced during that auspicious weekend led me to a life anew, eternally marked by a transforming light. Although still far from perfect, I've gained the knowledge of what truly matters in life. My perception of our world has also evolved since this period of enlightenment, as I now view each new day through a prism of *peace, hope and joy.*

Taking a new direction in life is far from a simple endeavor. To tell you the truth, it can be downright painful. At times, it feels like you're walking through fire, the intense flames of purification. At other, you feel the consuming chill of isolation – an agonizing reality. During my transformation, people that once loved me, turned their backs on me. Others would simply look away or were just too busy to be concerned. My motives, values, faith, and even my sanity became a point of contention. Followed by varied forms of persecution.

I forgave, and pray for those who persecuted me.

Today, I live a life near the United States poverty level. I do without many of the pleasures in life that I once considered necessities. I'm also living without many true necessities, like the almighty prescription card and basic healthcare coverage. There are times that I go without, rather than to ask for help.

Yet, from my *challenge* came an amazing endowment. The gift of empathy. I have captured a glimpse of life from my brother's reality, seeing the struggles that being without doles out. The old me would have considered such circumstances disastrous, unthinkable. But after looking into the eyes of children living without the basics to survive, clean water to drink or food to eat, I realized that I am truly blessed.

> *I know what it is to be in need, and I know what it is to have plenty. I have learned the secret of being content in any and every situation, whether well fed or hungry, whether living in plenty or in want. I can do everything through Him who gives me strength.*
> *- Philippians 4:4-7*

I'm blessed with a solid family network that loves me and would never let me go hungry. I'm blessed with friends that would stand by me, night and day. I've found *real love* among brothers and sisters, from all around this awesome world, who cared enough to share with me valuable life lessons. Because of such love shown to me, I now possess the *vision* to see *the least of these* as my family.

I am blessed, living on less, so that I may bless others. I chose to heed the call. I made a commitment to my Lord, a commitment to reach out to *all people* with His love. I became a messenger for the *New Revolution*.

Something's happening in our world. Take a look around. *Really* talk to one another. Find the courage to look beyond the circumstances that consume your daily life. Be honest with yourself. You're not the only one that's thinking it. Share your knowledge, your piece of our greater wisdom. Seek the winds of change, the spirit of the New Revolution moving among us. Our world is passing beyond the obvious, beyond the physical. We are entering an era of renewal, of hope – a day when the Spirit of God rules over the *rules of man.*

The *beginning* is near. We stand at the dawning of the day of awakening, called to pursue the collective wisdom of our unified love – a love that will alter our universe. Through such love, we can align with the spirits within *each one of us* to attain His revolutionary level of awareness. Remember, *through love, grow in knowledge and depth of insight.*

Insight can never be taught or legislated. Insight can only be gained through seeking, listening and living. Jesus teaches through parables, rather than *dictating* His wisdom. Anything worth obtaining requires effort and commitment. Seek and you will find; listen and you will hear.

Evil is the enemy we fight in these days of the new holy war. Extremists of every kind, from every nation, are drawing upon the forces of evil to wage this war. In the name of God and Sovereignty, their deceit moves freely among us to influence and manipulate, to mislead us down an evil path of destruction.

Something's gotta give. We're at a divine crossroads, a time of worlds colliding. The warfare orchestrated by the misguided, hypocritical, extremist sects of Isaac and Ishmael will not end until the coming of the new heavens and earth. We must peer more deeply into our existence. And we must participate more truthfully in our reality. The New Revolution requires that level of commitment. It requires our *action*.

By the will of God, the communal power of our unified love, evil can be conquered.

> *For Jesus is our peace; in his flesh he has made both groups into one and has broken down the dividing wall, that is, the hostility between us.*
>
> *- Ephesians 2:14-16*

This is the New Revolution [same as the Old Revolution], founded in absolute truth, the greatest commandment of all.

America now faces an epic challenge, a *Jihad*. Our enemy draws upon the rules of engagement that are only employed by a holy warrior. A battle fought, not with weapons of mass destructions, but within the soul. A battle that rages in the most unexpected place – the hearts of *each one of us*.

Be alert, evil is very deceiving.

> *Finally, be strong in the Lord and in his mighty power. Put on the full armor of God so that you can take your stand against the devil's schemes. For our struggle is not against flesh and blood, but against the rulers, against the authorities, against the powers of this dark world and against the spiritual forces of evil in the heavenly realms. Therefore put on the full armor of God, so that when the day of evil comes, you may be able to stand your ground, and after you have done everything, to stand. Stand firm then, with the belt of truth buckled around your waist,*

*with the breastplate of righteousness in place, and with your feet fitted with the readiness that comes from the gospel of peace. In addition to all this, take up the shield of faith, with which you can extinguish all the flaming arrows of the evil one. Take the helmet of salvation and the sword of the Spirit, which is the word of God. And pray in the Spirit on all occasions with all kinds of prayers and requests. With this in mind, be alert and always keep on praying for all the saints.*

*- Ephesians 6:10-18(NIV)*

If we truly take Jesus at His Word, freedom shall prevail. Freedom from worry, freedom from guilt, freedom from aggression, and even freedom from so much of the sin that fills our daily lives. Through such freedom, He will change our world.

Brothers and Sisters of the New Revolution, unite! Actively seek out one another. Smile. Wave. Flash a peace sign, our symbol of Victory. Create unity among us; community among us. Ask those you meet, *"Are we One?"* Seek the awareness of our *common spiritual consciousness*, made complete by the Spirit of God, the *Holy Spirit*. As you move among the challenges of our world, show particular concern for those who are brothers and sisters, while never neglecting to accept and care for those who are not. Show the love that *each one of us* has been given to share.

About Silvio. Sure, I've heard from him. At first, he was relentless in his pursuit. Thank God for Karim, a real brother. Without his help, the *Brotherhood* would surely have captured me. Now, Silvio appears on the scene much less often. Usually when I least expect it. No problem, I *just keep driving*. His unending quest to conquer me is no longer a real threat. I simply take it as a healthy reminder of those days.

A reminder that *I choose where I draw the line.*

May God's love be with you, my friend.

Always.

# Dedication

As the Father has loved me, so have I loved you. Now remain in my love. If you obey my commands, you will remain in my love, just as I have obeyed my Father's commands and remain in his love. I have told you this so that my joy may be in you and that your joy may be complete. My command is this: Love each other as I have loved you. Greater love has no one than this, that he lay down his life for his friends. You are my friends if you do what I command. I no longer call you servants, because a servant does not know his master's business. *Instead, I have called you friends*, for everything that I learned from my Father I have made known to you. You did not choose me, but I chose you and appointed you to go and bear fruit—fruit that will last. Then the Father will give you whatever you ask in my name.

This is my command: *Love each other.*

~ John 15:9-17 (NIV)

*In Loving Memory*

✝

*The Chief*

*Tim and Old School*

237

## The fine print.

If I offended you, it was honestly unintentional. This is a story that had to be told. You just happened to have the dumb luck of impacting my life. Or was it our destiny? God bless. –k

From the book: *Sights I See Within Me*
By: Richard Reynolds Montour *(a brother)*


I have it all figured out.
I know nothing.
I know nothing cause God did not give me the ability
           to pour blood out of my veins so fast
       that the past stops and speaks to me!

I have nothing.
No knowledge of the weak.
No determination for the week.
No affliction or addiction swaying me from way to way
     from day to day
        granting peace to angels
     as they speak and say that every soul is unique.

So I have it all figured out.
I have it within me, ready to discreetly secrete the ebony defeat
     of our blessed regime.
The presidential seat is so far beyond what the world believes to
be free, yet nobody goes out and consciously defeats
the position that fuels the greed.
Why do we constantly supply the arms with guns
     instead of speaking truth with our tongues?

I know nothing.
I know nothing of the repeat of the history of the war,
     or the core from where the violence comes from anymore.
I know of not where we come from, or where we want to go,
but I do know that the angel within me is stronger than a bullet.
   I do know that the voice that I hold is stronger than the gun
     as you pull it!
   I do know that the survival of a race is dependent upon grace,
     and kindness comes not enough, only two times
     from the sword that holds the steel cuffs!
Violence is wrong. It is wrong indeed. I hope today we can all be freed.
     So we can see that we know nothing.

## About the author...

Once a successful and driven businessman, today Kev lives a more adventurous and fulfilling life, while possessing *no fear* of death; for many reasons. No longer enticed by money or success, he now lives by a simple philosophy – love.

Having escaped to Northern Wisconsin in 2007 to write Eden, Kev now calls De Pere, Wisconsin home – a place where people are *real*. While lacking many of the amenities of urban life, *Les Rapides des Pères* (the rapids of the fathers) offers a rare and comforting glimpse into a time when Americans were truly free.

Although usually on the road, when in De Pere, Kev can likely be found pontificating at *Montagues Wine Bar and Café*.

www.kev.net

☮

NOTE: The author will contribute at least 50% of his financial gain from the sale of this book to support charitable causes and to serve brothers and sisters in need.

*I've discovered a secret along the way. It's far better to fear God than to fear one's self.*

*~k*

Printed in the United States
147269LV00005B/1/P